"You gave me an ultimatum. Either I marry you or we stop seeing each other."

"It wasn't an ultimatum!"

"We both know what you meant, don't we? Either I marry you or you won't sleep with me again."

Kit stared back, her face clenched in misery and anger.

"Yes, that's what I said," she agreed. "I want a man who loves me enough to want to live with me, a man who loves me enough to be ready to make a commitment to me.... Obviously that man isn't you!"

Dear Reader,

In this book I deal with the sin of Sloth. Sometimes when you've been under a terrible strain, it is vital to take time out, to let your physical and emotional bruises heal before getting back into life's struggles.

But there's another form of laziness. I picture this as the two-toed sloth, a comical, cuddly, furry animal, lumbering along a branch upside down, taking forever to get anywhere. It's a rather lovable creature and we all know someone who is prone to move like that, refusing to hurry, or make decisions, reluctant to take responsibility, putting off until tomorrow what they should do today. You can hurt someone you love, who loves you, by being slow to show how you feel; you might even lose them altogether.

Charlotte Lamb

Books by Charlotte Lamb

ALSO AVAILABLE IN HARLEQUIN PRESENTS
SINS

Charlotte Lamb

Hot Blood

Harlequin Books

TORONTO • NEW YORK • LONDON
AMSTERDAM • PARIS • SYDNEY • HAMBURG
STOCKHOLM • ATHENS • TOKYO • MILAN
MADRID • WARSAW • BUDAPEST • AUCKLAND

ISBN 0-373-11852-X

HOT BLOOD

First North American Publication 1996.

Copyright © 1996 by Charlotte Lamb.

Printed in U.S.A.

CHAPTER ONE

THE film ended suddenly and the house lights came up before Kit had time to pull herself together. She scrabbled in her bag for a handkerchief, her head bent so that her silvery hair half hid the tears streaming down her face.

She didn't want anyone to notice her. She felt stupid, sitting here in floods of tears over an old black and white movie made before most of the audience had even been born!

Kit was a film buff, obsessed with the cinema and with the techniques of filming; it was her hobby. She had a camcorder and often spent a weekend filming landscapes or recording amateur productions at the little local theatre in town. She particularly loved old black and white films. They had so much more atmosphere; a tension and power that films shot in colour simply didn't have, and possessed a sense of the past—a nostalgia—which she found irresistible.

When the Classic Film Club had opened at this small cinema, once known as the Flea Pit but now modernised and given the grandiose name of the Imperial—although everyone still called it the Flea Pit—Kit had immediately become a member. She wasn't so much interested in seeing the films themselves, which were mostly available on video now, but the club also had monthly lectures by film critics, directors, and actors; occasionally it even got hold of a rare old film which you wouldn't get on video.

People began pushing past her, hurrying to get home or into the Chinese restaurant across the road, which was always busy at this time of night.

'Excuse me!' they said impatiently, and Kit struggled to her feet to let them get by, trying to make herself very small, which wasn't difficult because she was only five feet two. She mumbled apologies, still clutching her handkerchief, pretending to be blowing her nose.

Only when the last one had filed past did she turn to follow, and that was when she realised that there was one other person still sitting in the row, in the seat next to her.

He was sitting sideways, arms folded, watching her, his long legs crossed, one foot swinging rhythmically, and he clearly had no intention of moving.

When their eyes met he murmured conversationally, as if they were old friends, 'I haven't seen a woman cry over a film for years. First time you've seen *Camille*?'

Kit felt herself go pink, and rather crossly nodded. Had he been watching her for long? She had been so engrossed in the film that she hadn't even noticed who was sitting next to her.

Giving him a rapid inspection, for a disconcerting instant she felt she knew him. There was something distinctly familiar about the set of his head, the rough brown hair silvered here and there by time, and the smiling, charming blue eyes. Or did he just resemble someone else? Who? She frowned, trying to remember, but the fleeting recognition had slipped away. Oh, well, maybe she'd come up with a name later.

'Is it the first time you've seen it too?' she asked, curious about him. He didn't look the type to love lushly romantic films, but then men could be deceptive. She had once had a short affair with a guy who had looked big and strong and dependable, and had been old enough to be all three, but had turned out to be tied to his mother's apron strings, incapable of doing a thing for himself, and about as tough as a paper hankie.

He gave her a charming, lazy smile. 'I can't remember how many times I've seen *Camille*. I'm a big Garbo fan. Are you? I've seen all her films over and over again but this one is my favourite. Have you read the book or seen the opera?'

Kit laughed until she saw from his face that he hadn't been joking. 'You mean there really is an opera?' she asked, her green eyes wide, glittering and sharp like shards of broken green glass in sunlight.

'*La Traviata*—have you ever seen that?'

She shook her head. 'I've heard of it, of course, but I'm not that keen on opera. I've never seen *La Traviata*, although I have heard the music quite often.'

'Oh, you'd love this opera—same storyline, more or less, but even sadder and more romantic than the film—but that's the music.' He smiled, and she blinked at how good-looking that smile made him.

His hair might have been going grey but his features were spare and rugged and his eyes held charm. 'Without music any film loses half its impact, don't you agree? You can do without words, but music creates the mood.'

Kit nodded. 'Absolutely. And they realised that right from the start of cinema. Even silent films were always accompanied by music—live music in that case, of course—a pianist or an organist. Even a trio, I gather, and—'

Behind them there was a meaningful cough, and Kit looked round and saw the cinema usherette, a pert blonde who wore a lot of make-up, impatiently tapping her foot and glaring. 'Oh, sorry! Are we the last to leave?'

'Yes, and we're waiting to lock up! Are you coming, or shall we leave you here all night?'

The girl turned on her heel and flounced off and Kit got up, grimacing. 'Oh, dear, she's cross now.'

The man stood up too, and immediately towered over her, making Kit feel smaller than ever as she followed him up the steps into the brightly lit foyer where the manager was waiting to lock up behind them.

'I was beginning to think you two planned to stay all night,' he told them in irritable tones.

'Sorry to keep you waiting; it was such a great evening's entertainment,' the tall man said, and gave him one of those smiles which changed his face. Kit watched the other man's features relax, saw an answering smile.

'Glad you enjoyed it, sir. We had an almost full house tonight; we always do for Garbo. Come again. Goodnight.'

'Goodnight,' they said, walking out through the big plate-glass doors which the manager locked behind them.

A cold March wind blew along the rain-wet street, and Kit shivered. Who would have thought that it was nearly spring? The passage of time had begun to depress her in recent years; it went too fast and she was worried by the speed with which the year flashed by. Am I getting old? she thought, and felt like breaking into a run, as though that would take her far away from such gloomy thoughts.

Before she could move, though, the tall man took hold of her coat collar and raised it so that it framed her face, sheltered her from the wind. She gave him a startled look, tensing at the feel of his gloved hands against her skin. 'What do you think you're doing?'

'You looked cold.' His hands still in position on either side of her head, he bent towards her and murmured, 'Fancy a Chinese meal?'

Kit's green eyes widened. 'You're a fast worker! I don't even know your name!'

'Don't be so Victorian!'

Oh, yes, he certainly had charm, she thought—a warm, lazy charm which showed most when his face was in motion, talking, laughing. He must have been a real drop-dead knockout when he was young. How old was he now? she wondered, eyeing him assessingly.

Younger than me, anyway, she decided. Not fifty yet. Getting on that way, but he looks good for his age. Men always did—that annoyed her whenever she thought about it. It was so unfair.

'Like what you see?' he asked, watching her watching him, his eyes bright as if he liked to have her looking at him.

'I'm thinking about it,' she told him tartly. She was no teenager to be swept off her feet by a stranger who tried to pick her up in a cinema! But she was flattered, she couldn't deny it. Maybe he was short-sighted and thought she was much younger than she actually was?

Who are you trying to kid? she cynically told herself. She probably looked older than her years! Along with all the other advantages they had, men aged slower than women. They didn't live as long, of course. Women tended to outlive them, but life did not compensate by letting women keep their looks into old age.

Time started in on you once you were in your forties, pencilling wrinkles in around your eyes and mouth, especially if you had ever smiled a lot, which seemed doubly unfair. Women with cold faces and cold hearts kept a smooth skin longer. If you were active, keen on skiing or sailing or just being out in the fresh air and sunshine, you paid for that too. I probably have skin like an old prune, she thought, remembering holidays in the sun, on boats and in Austria, skiing.

Oh, well, she had had a wonderful time during all those years, and she didn't regret a minute of it, but she avoided mirrors these days.

'Well, don't take too long making up your mind,' he drawled. 'Sorry to rush you, and I don't normally go this fast, but I don't want to let you go before I get a chance to find out more about you and make sure I am going to see you again.'

Kit was breathless and, for once, wordless. I know who he looks like! she thought at that instant. Clark Gable. All he needs is a moustache.

He gazed down into her eyes and said softly, 'I'll start by telling you I'm Joe Ingram. I'm forty-two, divorced, heterosexual; I've lived in a lot of different places, in a lot of different countries, and I've only just moved here, but I've suddenly decided I'm going to love it.'

Kit gave him an incredulous look. 'Is there anything wrong with your eyesight, Joe? For your information, I'm fifty-two—that's ten years older than you! I'm also divorced, I have a son of twenty-six who's married with two kids of his own, and my hair is silver where it used to be blonde.'

He put out a long forefinger and curled a strand of her hair around it. 'It's naturally silver? I thought you'd dyed it. It looks terrific—and you didn't tell me your name.'

'Kit—Kit Randall,' she said slowly, staring at him. 'Did you hear what I said? I'm ten years older than you.'

'I'm not deaf; of course I heard you. I'm not hung up on age. Are you? That's a very conventional attitude.'

'This is a very conventional little town, Joe. Most small towns are very hot on traditions and conventions—at least, in England they are; and Silverburn is no different. I know—I've lived here all my life.'

It seemed a terrible confession as she said it; he was clearly sophisticated, cosmopolitan, experienced, the very opposite of her quiet, stay-at-home self. She had never had the urge to go away from this tranquil, beautiful corner of England with its hedged green fields, deep, shady woods and ancient villages.

This town was very old too, with houses from every period of English history—medieval, Elizabethan, Georgian, Victorian and modern—all muddled up together and yet merging into a graceful whole, weathered by time and use.

Silverburn was a tourist attraction because a famous eighteenth-century poet had been born here, whose house was on the pilgrimage map, particularly for Americans since his son had emigrated there after his death. Silverburn was also a friendly little town, with a strong sense of identity. The local population of the town was small enough to have the necessary community spirit; people grew up here and stayed, hardly ever moved away the way Kit had.

She felt lucky to have been born here; she was very happy with her life, and yet suddenly she wondered if she was going to bore him, if he was going to find her dull compared with other women that he must have known in all those other places in which he had lived.

Curious, she asked him, 'What job do you do, Joe? Why have you lived in so many different countries?'

'I've been a photographer for years, working on an international magazine, and freelancing of late. Now I'm writing my autobiography; it will be quite short, I think, because I'm not much good with words; it will just be a commentary to go with a collection of my best pictures.'

'It sounds fascinating. Will I have seen any of your work?'

He shrugged. 'Maybe. That's enough about me—what about you? You forgot to say if you're free.'

She half wished she could say yes, she was, but she shook her head, her mouth level and regretful.

'No, not really.'

He grimaced. 'Sorry to hear that. I suppose you remarried after the divorce?'

'No, I'm not married! And you ask too many questions!' Suddenly angry, she began to walk away fast and he caught up with her.

'Sorry if I upset you. Look, it isn't really late! Come for a coffee across the street. Please.'

Kit hesitated, then a little reluctantly shook her head. 'Sorry. I must get home.'

'To a man?'

She looked all the way up at him, green eyes wide, startled and laughing. 'You do believe in being direct, don't you?'

'No time to be anything else once you're over forty!'

She laughed again. 'True. No, I don't live with anyone.' As she heard herself say it she also heard an echo deep inside her—a sadness, a regret. She lived alone and she hated it more every day. She was lonely and she ached to have a real home again, someone to come home to, someone who cared whether she came home or not. It was dreary going back to a dark, empty flat and going to bed alone.

'Then if there's nobody waiting up for you, come and have a coffee,' said Joe firmly, pushing his hand between her arm and her body and urging her across the street to where a new, modern coffee-bar was brightly lit and full of young people talking and laughing and drinking coffee.

Kit lagged behind, staring at all those intent, alive young faces and feeling out of it, old, left behind. 'I really shouldn't.'

'Why not?'

'I don't know a thing about you.'

'You know a lot about me,' he argued. 'You know my name, how old I am, that I'm a lonely stranger here, and that I love Greta Garbo. And anyway, what on earth could I do to you in a coffee-bar full of other people?'

Kit was very tempted. But it would be reckless to accept—whatever he said, she knew very little about him.

Of course, she found him attractive. He had a powerful, firm body under his clothes—you could tell that just by the way he walked—and his eyes had a naughty twinkle, like a little boy's. He obviously liked life, and she liked the way he dressed too—casually but with style, in good brown checked tweeds, a cream shirt, no tie, with a bright red silky scarf hanging round his neck inside his open camel-hair winter coat. And he had such a charming smile.

But her small-town mind wouldn't let her take the risk easily. How did she even know that Joe Ingram was really his name, or that he wasn't married with three point five children? Yet she wanted to go on talking to him; she was enjoying his company and she was reluctant to say goodbye; she couldn't deny it.

What can he do to you in a coffee-bar? she asked herself impatiently. Don't be such an idiot.

'So long as you let me pay for my own coffee,' she finally said, and he grinned at her in amusement.

'The independent type! Well, that's fine by me. I'm certainly not going to argue.'

As they walked across the road she looked sideways at him, measuring his height beside her, a little daunted by it, and wondering if his overcoat was cashmere—nothing else looked that soft and fine, did it? The tweed suit was well-worn and a little shabby, yet it must have cost quite a bit when it was new.

'Do you actually live in Silverburn?' she asked him, and he nodded, glancing down at her.

'I've just moved into a flat in Townwall Street.'

She stiffened and gave him another startled look as he held the door of the coffee-bar open for her.

'Really? That's where I live—I've got a flat on the first floor of the big new apartment block right next to the entrance to the new shopping centre.'

He halted, staring down at her. 'Snap! My flat is on the top floor—number fourteen. What an amazing coincidence.' His blue eyes were almost dark in the brighter lights.

Kit felt quite odd about it. She didn't believe in fate but it was a very big coincidence that they should have run into each other in a cinema like that. Or was it? Had he seen her going in or out of the building? Had he followed her to the cinema tonight? Or recognised her in the cinema and deliberately picked her up like that?

She had thought he looked familiar, she recalled. She must have seen him without really noticing him. It hadn't just been that fleeting, fugitive resemblance to Clark Gable that had struck her.

If he had told her he lived in the same block of flats she probably wouldn't have agreed to have coffee with him; she would have suspected his motives. But she couldn't get out of it now.

They found a small table right in the corner and sat down. The noise was deafening; a jukebox was playing near the bar and the other customers yelled at each other over the deep beat of rock music.

A young waitress chewing gum came over, pad in one hand, pencil in the other, and stared at them indifferently.

'Yes?'

'Two coffees, please,' Joe said, smiling at her.

'Anything else?' She didn't smile back, just chewed her gum.

'No, thank you.'

The girl walked away. Joe gave Kit a wry grin. 'Maybe we should have gone to the pub instead. It might not have been so noisy.'

'Noisier tonight,' Kit assured him. 'There's a darts match on; they're playing their rival pub; it could get very nasty.'

'You drink there?' He looked surprised.

'I sometimes eat my lunch there on weekdays— they do very good food. Doreen, the landlady, was at school with me.'

The waitress came back and dumped their coffees on the table. 'Will you pay me now? We're closing in fifteen minutes and we want to cash up the till.'

Kit began to get out her purse, but Joe had already given the girl a handful of coins. 'Keep the change,' he said.

'Thanks,' she said, with the first flicker of a smile, and walked away again.

Kit offered him the price of her coffee. He shook his head. 'You can pay next time.'

'Who says there's going to be a next time?' But she put her purse back into her handbag.

'I hope there will.' He looked at her seriously and she looked down, flushing. He was giving her butterflies in her stomach, and it was a very long time since a man had done that to her. She didn't know how to answer him.

After a pause he asked, 'Do you have a job?'

'I work for the local auctioneer, Keble's.'

'Doing what?'

'I help in most departments. I take auctions, I price antiques and paintings, work on the accounts, even help with packing up items for posting if we're short-handed.'

'You must be very clever. Have you had years of training?'

'Not exactly. I did an art degree before I got married, and my father ran an antiques shop, so I picked up quite a bit from him. I worked in the shop with him after I got married, to earn some extra money while my son was small.

'I kept up my studies in the evenings, while Paul was asleep; I read a good deal and I took evening classes. I managed to get to London quite often to visit museums and art galleries. My husband was an expert in Oriental ceramics; he taught me a great deal too. I inherited my father's personal collection of English furniture and porcelain when he died, so I suppose in one way or another I've been studying antiques all my life.'

Joe leaned his elbows on the table, sipping his coffee while he stared at her, his blue eyes narrowed and thoughtful. She stared back, prickling at the fixed nature of his gaze, and when he still didn't speak said after a minute, 'What? What?'

'What what?' he repeated, laughing.

'What are you thinking?' she asked him crossly.

He put out a finger and flicked it down her cheek, his voice soft. 'That your hair is like spun silver and when you're full of enthusiasm your face lights up as you talk.'

She went pink. 'Oh, stop it! I'm not a teenager to be flattered like that.' She took a sip of her own coffee; it was lukewarm by now. It couldn't have been very hot to start with.

'How long have you been divorced?'

Another of his abrupt, direct questions. 'Five years,' she said. 'What about you?'

'I can't even remember. She left me years ago—said she was sick of being married to a man she never saw, and I can't blame her; I was always out of the country. She thought my job was dangerous, too.'

'Was it?'

He laughed. 'In a way—if you were in the wrong place at the wrong time, but luckily I never was. Oh, I had a few little accidents—broke a leg once, got shot in the shoulder, got blown off my feet and spent a few weeks with concussion and a touch of deafness in one ear—but—'

'But nothing serious,' Kit drily concluded for him, and he grinned at her, amusement in his blue eyes.

'Well, I survived it all, let's put it like that.'

'Let's,' she agreed. 'What on earth made you choose Silverburn to move to after this peaceful life of yours? Do you think you're ready for the heady excitements of our bustling metropolis?'

Quite seriously he said, 'I was sick of flying around the world, sick of wars and famines, sick of city life, very sick of daily tension. I wanted to get out into the English countryside, and I had an aunt who lived here once, when I was just a kid. I

remembered it as a lovely town, full of old buildings
and great shops, and close to some gorgeous
countryside too—so I came to look it over and decided it would suit me down to the ground.'

The waitress was banging a saucepan on the
counter. 'Closing time!' she yelled. 'Go home, all
of you!'

Grumbling, the other customers began to get up,
put on coats, fasten their buttons, before drifting
out into the night.

Joe and Kit followed. They were the last customers; the waitress locked up behind them.

'Can I give you a lift? My car is parked over
behind the cinema,' Joe offered.

'I came in my own car,' Kit said, walking purposefully towards the same cinema car park. The
street was almost empty now; the teenagers from
the coffee-bar were running to catch a late-night
bus, everyone from the cinema had gone home and
there was very little traffic at this time of night.

The town was going to sleep, and she was very
conscious of being alone with a stranger. It was an
experience she had not had since her own teens,
which were so long ago that it gave her vertigo to
remember that far back.

Joe fell into step with her without haste, his
strides longer. 'How about dinner tomorrow? I'll
book a table in advance so we won't have a
problem. Have you got a favourite restaurant? I
haven't had time to check them all out yet; you'll
have to advise me.'

'I'm rather busy, I'm afraid. Sorry.' Kit reached her little red Ford and stooped to unlock the door, not looking at him. 'Goodnight,' she said quickly, sliding into the driver's seat and pulling the door shut.

He bent down and tapped on the window. She touched the button which made the glass slide down and looked warily at him.

'What changed your mind?' he asked, his face wry.

She decided to be as blunt in return. 'I told you, I'm not free; I already have a man in my life.'

'And it's serious?'

'Yes, it's serious,' she said, meeting his eyes levelly. 'Goodnight.'

He had his hand on the glass and had to snatch it back as the window silently closed again. The engine started. Kit put her foot down and drove off, leaving him standing there, staring at her. Something in the way he watched her made the hair prickle on the back of her neck.

There was almost no other traffic about, so she was able to drive quite fast, yet as she drew up at the traffic lights at the end of the high street she saw a sleek black Porsche pull in behind her. Kit looked at it idly in her driving mirror, envying the style and potential speed, then stiffened as she recognised the driver. He raised a hand in greeting.

Kit waved back briefly, but her heartbeat had speeded up and she felt her nerves jumping as she drove on.

Oh, stop it! Of course he's driving the same way; he's going to the same block of flats, isn't he? she told herself impatiently. What's the matter with you? Does he look dangerous? She flicked another glance into the mirror to watch the Porsche following right on her tail.

Photography obviously paid well. His clothes looked expensive and his car certainly did. He must have earned a good deal if he could afford a Porsche! Was he famous? Should she have heard of him? She knew very little about anything outside her own chosen sphere of interest. Antiques were the only things she knew much about.

In her eagerness to get away from him, to get home, she was driving too fast. As she turned the next corner she almost hit another car coming out of a side road.

Tyres screeched, a horn blared, and Kit got a glimpse of a furious, alarmed face before the other car was lost from sight behind her. She slowed down after that and behind her the black Porsche slowed too.

She shot a look into her mirror and saw his reflection in it; the gleam of amused blue eyes, the cynical mouth. There was something about him— something disturbing; she had sensed it from the minute she'd set eyes on him but hadn't been sure what it was she saw or felt.

She had thought she recognised him, and perhaps she had seen him before going in or out of the block of flats, or maybe it was just that faint resemblance to Clark Gable she had picked up on, but she suspected that she had also been reacting instinctively to the man himself. He had charm and he was attractive and he was certainly persistent—but there was a sense of threat from him too. He worried her, and she had enough emotional problems in her life already. She didn't need another one.

The chief thing on her mind at the moment, though, was getting back home before he could beat her to it. She wasn't going to relax until she was safely in her flat with the door locked.

The block of flats had an underground car park. Kit had always hated parking there at night, walking through the dimly lit vault of the basement to the lift to go up to her flat, and tonight was no exception. She was desperate to get there before the man driving behind her.

She shot down the steep slope, parked in her numbered space without worrying about doing it perfectly, jumped out, hearing the Porsche smoothly reversing into another space nearby, locked her car and ran for the lift as if she were training for the Olympics.

She was lucky. The lift doors opened as soon as she touched the button; she leapt inside and jabbed the button for her floor, silently praying that they would close before Joe Ingram could catch up with her.

The doors closed. Kit breathed a sigh of relief. The lift went up and stopped, the doors opened and she walked out, her keyring swinging from her finger, then she stopped dead in shock.

Joe Ingram was leaning on the wall, waiting for her. 'What took you so long?' his voice drawled, and he laughed at her stunned expression.

He must have run up the stairs but he wasn't out of breath. It was Kit who was having to drag air into her lungs, her heart beating twice as fast as normal.

'Look, can't you get the message—?' she began, but he interrupted.

'I only wanted to say that if you ever changed your mind and wanted to see me again I'd give you my phone number,' he drawled, looking amused, his blue eyes teasing, and she felt stupid. She had overreacted, so now she tried to sound calm and reasonable.

'No, sorry; I won't change my mind. Goodnight.'

'At least take my card,' he said, pushing a printed card into her hand.

She was tempted to drop it on the floor, but if she did he would probably only give her another one. Irritably she pushed the card into her coat pocket.

'Is this a recent affair?' he asked, his body casually at ease as he leaned on the wall. 'I mean, how long have you known this guy?'

Very flushed and angry, she bit out, 'Honestly, you take the biscuit! I'm not telling you all about my private life!'

'I'm just trying to work it out. You aren't living with him yet you say it's serious, and tonight you were on your own—why wasn't he with you? Does that mean it's serious for you but not for him?'

She felt a stab of pain because he had hit on the truth and it hurt. 'Mind your own business!' She wasn't answering his questions, however close he came to guessing the truth. She had no intention of telling him anything more about herself; he already knew too much and she didn't like the way he had chased her up here.

'Don't get cross, Kit,' he said reproachfully.

'I'm tired. Goodnight,' she said, sidestepping him, not sure what she would do if he wouldn't let her walk away. Her nerves jangled as she took her first step.

But he didn't stop her; he just turned and watched her go, then said softly, 'Do I need references?'

She ignored him. As she reached her door and put her key into the lock he said, 'Goodnight, then, Kit. See you again soon!' And then she heard the door to the stairs banging behind him, the sound of his feet running up the stairs.

Although Kit was tired and went straight to her bedroom, washed and was in bed in about ten minutes, she didn't get to sleep for another half an hour.

She kept thinking about him, going over everything he had said to her, remembering every look on his face, every glance from those vivid blue eyes.

She had never met a man who had made such a deep impression at first sight and she hoped she would be able to put him out of her mind; she certainly meant to forget him as fast as she could. He wasn't even her type.

She didn't like men who played games in the way she sensed he did. How many other women had he chased the way he'd just chased her? What was his success rate?

It worried her that she had immediately been attracted to him without knowing a thing about him. It wasn't like her; it was completely out of character. She had told him that she was the cautious type and it was true. Kit had always preferred to look before she leapt, even when she'd been young.

She and Hugh had known each other for years before they'd got married. She couldn't blame the failure of their marriage on too much haste in the beginning. They had been teenagers when they'd met, and had taken six years to get to the altar. They had both been so very sensible. No doubt that was why, at the age of forty-five, Hugh had suddenly lost his head over a girl half his age and run off with her one night without warning.

For the first time in his entire life Hugh had acted on impulse, had let emotion rule him, and once Kit had got over the shock she had come to feel a certain sympathy for him. Their divorce had been entirely amicable and they had stayed friends—at a distance.

Hugh and his bride, Tina, had gone off to live in Germany, near Tina's family. He now worked for a museum in Bonn, heading its ceramics department. He was brilliant at his job; he had a strong international reputation and could identify an object almost at a glance.

Hugh liked living in Germany, and he got on well with his colleagues. Cool-headed, logical, sensible in everything except the way he felt about his new wife, Tina, and their little blonde twin girls, aged two now, he was happier now than he had ever been in his life before.

Kit had met them all last summer when they'd visited England to see her son, Paul, and his family. She had been struck by how happy Hugh had looked and had been glad—she felt no bitterness towards him.

If she had really loved him she would have done, presumably—but had she? she wondered, yawning, and couldn't be sure. She barely remembered the way she had felt in her teens. A very different emotion had blotted out everything that went before it, had made all other love pale into insignificance. Now she really understood her ex-husband in a way she hadn't done before. When real love hit you everything else vanished.

But she wouldn't think about that. She had to get some sleep. She had a busy day ahead tomorrow.

She thought about work instead, and slowly fell asleep.

Next day she was up very early. She showered, dressed in an elegant, pale coffee-coloured silk dress, blow-dried her hair into its usual style, had coffee, orange juice and a slice of toast, and at eight o'clock was waiting for Paddy and Fred to pick her up in their van, which was crammed so full of antiques that she had to sit squeezed into the front with them.

'Sorry there isn't much room,' Fred apologised, so close that she was almost on his lap as he drove. 'I brought everything I thought we might sell.'

'And then some,' said Paddy, grinning.

'Well, you never know!' Fred defiantly told her. He was a gentle giant of a man; over six feet, curly-haired, with broad shoulders and huge hands that were astonishly deft and sensitive.

By contrast Paddy was even smaller than Kit, barely five feet tall, tiny and fragile-looking, yet she had a muscular strength that belied her size, and could carry heavy furniture or packing cases for miles if required.

They weren't married but they were planning a wedding in just six weeks and meanwhile were getting a home together in an old terraced cottage down near the river. Kit had often had supper there with them, helping out with their work on the cottage before they ate a meal together—usually a casserole slow-cooked in the oven by Paddy for hours.

They had hardly any furniture yet. They were both keen on do-it-yourself—Paddy was a marvel with a sewing machine and had made all the curtains and chair covers; Fred had done some of the plumbing, and was putting in a fitted kitchen and building a wall-to-wall wardrobe in the bedroom.

They worked on their future home at weekends, and of course their furniture was all antique—not necessarily very valuable, but always well made and handsome to look at. Paddy could pick up objects for a song and refurbish them—mending chair legs, replacing torn materials, French-polishing surfaces that had been scarred or rubbed away.

Kit's partner, Liam Keble, was proposing to give them a Victorian bedroom set that he had noticed them coveting in the shop—tallboy, bed and dressing-table, all mahogany, in very good condition. Paddy and Fred had been over the moon when he'd told them it would be their wedding present.

Paddy had hugged Liam. Fred had kissed Kit, hugging her so enthusiastically that he had almost crushed her ribs.

'I suppose Liam's meeting us at the market?' asked Paddy, breaking in on Kit's thoughts.

She nodded. 'I imagine so; he didn't say he wouldn't be there.'

He wasn't saying anything to her at all but she didn't tell Paddy that, although the other woman had undoubtedly noticed the atmosphere between the two partners.

Liam lived in an elegant Georgian house on the edge of town, a few minutes from the little village where today's market was being held in an old school. The early Victorian building was sited beautifully, looking down over the village of Great Weatherby, and framed by trees and fields.

As they drove towards it Kit thought how wonderful it must have been for small children to start learning in such surroundings, where their parents and grandparents and great-grandparents had all gone before them. No wonder local people had been up in arms over the loss of their school, but there had only been sixty-odd pupils, and however violently parents had protested they had been defeated by economics.

Now the children all went by bus to the next village, some three miles away, and the old village school was to be sold. In the meantime it was being used for a monthly market in antiques and second-hand furniture.

When Fred drove into the school car park the yard was already crowded with cars—mostly other dealers who had got there early.

Fred began moving the heavier items while Kit carried a box of lighter objects into the high-ceilinged old Victorian hall.

As she walked in she heard a deep voice and her heart turned over instantly. Liam!

Her green eyes searched for him among the crowds of people milling about. He was standing beside one stall, picking up a delicate French clock which, even at this distance, she registered as nine-teenth century and exquisitely enamelled. His black head gleamed in the watery sunlight streaming down from arched windows set high in the panelled walls.

Kit looked at him with pain and yearning, walking towards him, waiting for him to see her. They had quarrelled a week ago and Liam was still furious. How would he look at her today?

For two years he had been her entire life, but Kit wasn't sure how much she meant to him, and it was eating her up.

'How about dinner tonight?' she suddenly heard him ask and stopped in her tracks, staring at the woman behind the stall that he was visiting.

'Dinner?' the woman repeated, smiling a curling little smile.

Kit had never seen her before. Slender, elegant, with dark red hair styled in light, waving ringlets, she had a pre-Raphaelite look to her, and a cool, acquisitive face too, with a witchy, pointed chin and sharp, cat-like yellowing eyes.

'There's a very good French restaurant in the market square in Silverburn,' Liam murmured.

'Is there? I love French food. I haven't discovered many of the local restaurants since I moved here. I'd love to have dinner tonight, Liam.'

Kit felt sick suddenly. She can't be much above thirty, she thought. She's young and beautiful, and Liam is staring at her as if she's what he's been looking for all his life. I know that mesmerised look—I saw it in Hugh's face when he fell for his blonde.

When Hugh had walked out on her for a younger woman it hadn't hurt like this, though. Nothing in her life had ever hurt like this.

CHAPTER TWO

LIAM turned and saw Kit a second later. His smile died instantly to be replaced by a frown. She wasn't surprised—he had been scowling at her for days— but it still saddened her, angered her too—how dared he look at her like that? It wasn't she who was behaving like a spoilt child, wanting to have everything its own way. But then wasn't that just like a man?

She looked at him with love and anger, wanting to smack him hard. His well-brushed black hair showed only fine streaks of silver although he was fifty himself now; it wasn't fair, thought Kit, wishing she didn't feel that deep surge of emotion just looking at him. Why did men retain their looks long after women's had begun to fade? Liam didn't look fifty. He was still lean and vibrant—a tall man with powerful shoulders, long legs and a lot of energy.

Paddy whispered to her, 'Oops! Someone's in a bad temper again! Whatever is the matter with him these days?'

Kit didn't tell her. She couldn't possibly have confided in Paddy—in anyone. The quarrel between her and Liam was too private to be talked about. It would be humiliating for anyone else to know about it.

Liam said goodbye to the woman he had been talking to and came over to them, his pale grey eyes glittering with ice as he held up his wrist and pointed to his watch.

'What time do you call this?'

Kit pondered the question, staring at his gold Cartier watch, which she knew had been a twenty-first birthday present to him from his father thirty years ago. It was still as beautiful as it must have been then, but Gerald Keble had been dead for twenty years. Was that part of the power of antiques—that they outlasted those who had created them or owned them? Or was it more that they somehow carried the patina of the times they had lived through, their surfaces polished by love over generations?

'Are we late?' she began, pretending not to be sure of it, and Liam's face tightened. He wasn't fooled by her wide-open eyes and surprised expression. He knew her too well.

'You know damned well you are! You should have been here half an hour ago! Every other stall was set up and doing business by half eight. Why weren't you here? I was; I was here by twenty past eight—where were you?'

She abandoned innocence in favour of defiance. 'Fred's van can only do forty miles an hour when it's loaded down with stuff, you know that! It might break down altogether if he pushed it.'

Fred and Paddy became very busy, not wishing to get drawn into the battle. They didn't enjoy confrontation or argument; they liked life to be peaceful, and Kit sympathised—she would rather have had a peaceful life too, but Liam was making that impossible for both of them.

'You should have left earlier!' he accused.

'We left early enough—but there was a lot of traffic on the road!'

'You should have made allowances for that.'

It was never easy to argue with Liam; he had an answer for everything. She looked at him furiously, her green eyes glittering. 'This is just wasting time! I've got better things to do than stand here bickering with you!'

As she turned away Liam tersely demanded, 'Where were you all last night?'

She froze, staring up at him. 'What?'

'Don't give me that innocent look! I know you weren't home. I wanted to remind you to get here by half past eight. I kept ringing from six-thirty onwards but just got your answering machine. I left a couple of messages asking you to ring me back, but you never did.'

Fred and Paddy had discreetly deposited their loads on the empty stall and melted away back to the van to get some more of the items they had brought, hoping no doubt that by the time they got back here she and Liam would have stopped snarling at each other. Some hope!

Turning her back on him, Kit began to unpack some of the wrapped pieces in one of the boxes, setting them out carefully on the stall. She felt Liam glaring at her as she unwrapped a piece of art nouveau glass—a twisty candlestick in rainbow colours which had been allowed to run like melting wax.

Casually without looking at him, she said over her shoulder, 'I went to the cinema club to see Garbo in *Camille* last night.'

'Was it a midnight performance?' he bit out.

'Midnight performance?' she repeated, baffled. 'Of course not!' She couldn't actually remember what time she had got back to her flat, but it hadn't been that late, surely?

She went on unwrapping porcelain, talking without looking at him. 'I was back home by midnight! I didn't check my answering machine; I forgot it was on so I didn't think of switching it off, and this morning I was in such a rush, grabbing some coffee and toast, that I still didn't remember to check to see if there were any messages. I went straight to bed as soon as I got home last night.'

'Did you go alone?' he asked, his tone as cutting as a knife going through silk.

Kit gave him an incredulous, angry stare. 'To bed?' She couldn't believe he had asked her that. Hot colour rushed up her face—the scarlet of rage rather than embarrassment.

'No, to the cinema!' he bit out like someone snapping cotton between their teeth.

'Yes to both, as it happens!' she snapped back. What was he suggesting—that she had gone out with someone else last night? Was having an affair? He was reacting with possessive jealousy, yet he kept saying that he didn't want to own her or have her own him. Why didn't he make up his mind? He

was the most contradictory, bewildering man she
had ever known.

'Really?' His mouth twisted cynically,
disbelievingly.

She hated the way he was looking at her. 'Believe
it or not, just as you like! It doesn't bother me,'
she muttered. 'Look, are you going to stand there
and watch me working? Would it be too much to
ask you to help?'

His face tight, he took a set of six French silver
dessert spoons out of the box and put them down
on the stall in a prominent place, his long fingers
automatically caressing even in his temper. Liam
loved beautiful things; he and Kit had that in
common, which was why their partnership had
worked so well until now.

He had inherited the auction rooms from his
father, Gerald Keble. He had worked for the firm
ever since he'd left university with an art degree
two years after Kit had graduated. Kit had been
engaged to Hugh by then and hadn't quite made
up her mind what she was going to do for a career.
She had worked in her father's shop until she'd got
married and had her son, and even while she was
running a home and taking care of Paul she had
still managed to work part-time for her father
during his lifetime.

It wasn't until later that she'd begun working with
Liam, but she had always known him through the
auction rooms which she and her father had frequently visited to buy objects for their shop. His
family—on both sides—had lived in Silverburn for

centuries; their names, many covered in moss and fading, were carved on rows of graves in the old churchyard behind St Mary's, the medieval church which stood on the top of the winding high street, as were those of Kit's ancestors.

Neither of them came from rich or powerful stock. They were descended from shopkeepers and market traders, farm labourers and wagoners—the ordinary working people of this little English town over many generations.

'I saw Mrs Walton, the vicar's wife, just now,' Liam murmured as he set out a Waterford crystal rose bowl on the stall. 'She told me she saw you last night coming out of the cinema with what she described as a very attractive man, much younger than you!'

Kit swallowed, going a furious shade of fuchsia. She should have known that someone was bound to notice her with Joe. This was a small town— anyone who had lived here for years knew almost everyone else; nothing you did was ever missed and people were always curious, and always talked about anything they saw or heard. You couldn't hope to keep a secret here.

That was, paradoxically, one of the things she loved about the place for all that it made her cross too; there was no chance of being forgotten or ignored here, of leading a lonely existence. You were part of the community whether you liked it or not and your entire life was an open book. That might have had a down side but it also made you feel good; you knew you belonged.

'I may have come out with him—I didn't go in there with him!' she said irritably, and then her heart suddenly began to beat like an overwound clock.

Was Liam jealous? The idea made her mouth go dry. Jealousy would mean that he cared—really cared. Or would it? He could just resent her showing signs of interest in someone else, even though he made it clear that there was no future for her with him. Men could be very dog-in-the-manger.

'Oh, I see,' he drawled sarcastically. 'You picked him up inside, did you?

'"Picked him up"?' she repeated, very flushed. 'I did nothing of the kind!'

He looked at her with a curling lip, contempt in his eyes, in his voice.

'What on earth's the matter with you? Don't you realise that a woman of your age is taking a stupid risk talking to a strange man in a cinema—especially if it's someone much younger than you? Mrs Walton said she was sure he wasn't even forty yet!'

Indignantly Kit said, 'Well, Mrs Walton's as wrong about his age as she is about most things! You'd think a vicar's wife would have more to do with her time than spread gossip. Joe's forty-two, as it happens! Not that much younger than me!' She had told Joe that she was much older than he was, but she didn't enjoy knowing that other people had thought the same thing.

Liam faced her, his eyes narrowed and hostile. 'Ten years younger, Kit! If it was the other way around, if you were ten years younger than him, it wouldn't matter so much but—'

'Why is it OK for a man to go out with a much younger woman but not the other way around?' she seethed, remembering the beautiful redhead he had been talking to—apparently it was OK for him to ask *her* out although she was twenty years younger than he was. 'If Joe doesn't mind me being older, what business is it of yours?'

His hard grey eyes glittered. 'You seem to know a lot about him. He wasn't a stranger, then? You'd met him before? How long have you known him?'

'What is this—the Spanish Inquisition?'

Liam coldly demanded, 'Why don't you want to talk about him? What have you got to hide?'

'I just don't like being grilled as if I were a murder suspect! As it happens, Joe lives in my apartment block.' She wasn't telling him the absolute truth— not because she was ashamed of it but because with Liam in his present mood she wasn't going to admit that she had let Joe pick her up in the cinema. She still couldn't believe it herself; even as a teenager she had never been one to strike up instant relationships.

But so what? It wasn't a crime, and Joe had been nice; she had been in no danger from him. She had known that from the minute they had got into conversation.

'He's a neighbour of yours?' Liam repeated, his frown etching heavy lines in his forehead. 'Have I seen him?'

'No, I don't think so. He's just moved here.'

'Where from?'

'Well ... London, I suppose.'

'You suppose? You mean you don't know where he came from?'

'He seems to have lived all over the world, but I think he was based in London.'

'You think? Well, what does he do for a living?'

'He retired recently—'

'Been sacked, you mean!' interrupted Liam roughly. 'If he's only forty he can hardly have retired! He's lost his job—and he's lying about it. I don't like the sound of that.'

Kit was getting angrier. 'Don't make such snap judgements! You've never even set eyes on him. He used to be a photographer on an international magazine, covering wars and revolutions, but he got tired of the life and gave up his job. He wasn't sacked or made redundant. He wanted to stop travelling, settle down somewhere; he's writing his autobiography.'

Liam's brows shot up. 'He's what? Writing his autobiography? He has to be kidding. You're very naïve if you swallowed that! Only famous people write their autobiographies—is he famous?' His voice was hard with sarcasm. 'What did you say his name was?'

'Joe Ingram.'

'Joe Ingram?' Liam's face changed, his eyes surprised. After a moment he said roughly, 'Well, I've heard of him. He got some sort of award last year for a photo of a dying soldier in an African street. It was a damned good picture—black and white. I saw it in an exhibition in London.' There was a pause, then he reluctantly muttered, 'I must say I was impressed.' He looked as if he hated to admit it.

Kit wished that she had seen it; it must have been good if it had impressed Liam; it wasn't easy to impress him. She wasn't surprised to hear that Joe had been very successful in his job, though—not only because he had told her that he was writing his autobiography but because there had been something assured and confident about the man himself. Joe was easy in his own skin; he had done a great deal, seen a lot of the world and found out about himself too, she suspected; found out enough to know what he wanted from life.

So many people led blinkered lives, blind to what they were doing or why—lives of fantasy, unaware of themselves or conscious of making the wrong choices. Discovering that you had taken a wrong turning in your life and firmly changing course was the act of an adult in touch with his own inner self.

That was what Hugh had done when he'd met Tina. He had turned his back on his entire existence until that moment and gone off bravely to a new life. Kit admired her ex-husband for that and didn't blame him. You only had one life. You had to live it for yourself, not other people; it did nobody any

good if you wasted your entire life being unhappy.
In fact, your unhappiness seeped into the lives of
those around you and made them unhappy too.

'Joe's publishing a series of photos in his book;
maybe that will be one of them,' she thought aloud.

'You've never mentioned him before,' Liam said
slowly, watching her. 'How long have you known
him?'

She gave him a quick, evasive glance and
shrugged. 'Oh, not long.'

Her mind raced feverishly—what was going on?
Why was Liam so angry? Why all these hostile
questions? She had known him most of her life,
just as she had her husband. Kit's world was a small
one; the people in it rarely altered year by year, day
by day, and she liked it like that. She was
comfortable with herself and her world.

Yet Liam was still mysterious to her, his responses and emotions as indecipherable as some
ancient script scratched on a primitive artefact. You
could sometimes make out a line here or there, but
the meaning of the whole defeated you. In fact she
was sure that he did not want her to know too much
about him; sometimes she even thought that he was
afraid of her getting too close. But why?

Paddy and Fred came back and began setting out
the furniture they had just carried into the hall.
Paddy set to work, energetically giving a plainly
decorated eighteenth-century country linen chest a
final polish to make it shine under the strong lights
of the hall. Fred checked that each item was marked
with the price, to forestall arguments with cus-

tomers, and made sure that the more expensive pieces were placed well to the back of the stall for safety's sake. You often got light-fingered customers looking for small, portable objects to walk off with while your attention was distracted by someone else. You had to have your wits about you, working in an antiques market.

'Paddy, look after the stall; we're going for a cup of coffee,' Liam said brusquely, grabbing Kit's arm as she opened her mouth to argue.

A moment later he was pulling her towards the exit and out into the watery gleam of March sunlight. Across the street from the village school stood the Blue Lion, a solidly built gabled pub from the eighteenth century.

This was where all the antiques dealers and their customers gathered for a traditional English breakfast on these cold mornings. The back room of the pub where the landlady cooked bacon and egg and made crisp golden toast and hot, strong coffee or tea was as crowded as usual. There were no free tables.

'We'll take our coffee outside, Mrs Evans,' Liam told the landlady, who handed him two brimming mugs.

'Sit in the snug, dear,' she said, glancing quickly from one to the other of them. 'Too cold to go outside.'

'Thanks,' he said, smiling down at her, and she went pink with pleasure.

Flirt! thought Kit bitterly, watching him turn on the charm that could make her own head spin on her shoulders.

The snug bar was a small, red-plush-upholstered room with a counter shining with highly polished brass. Liam put down the mugs of coffee on a black marble-topped table and sat on one of the red plush seats, stretching out his long legs as Kit sank down next to him.

'Why have we come over here?' she asked.

'To talk without witnesses.' He turned towards her, his profile hard. 'Let's have the truth, shall we? Are you dating Joe Ingram to stick a knife in me?'

She drew a long, shaky breath. 'What are you talking about?'

His voice was angry. 'You know damned well what I'm talking about! A few days ago you asked me to marry you and I was honest enough to tell you that I never wanted to get married again. I thought you were adult enough to take the truth, but I guess women never are.'

Face burning, she angrily said, 'I did not ask you to marry me! All I said was were we going to get married some time or did you intend to go on for ever the way we've been for the past year?'

His mouth twisted cynically. 'Don't play games with words, Kit. You asked me if I was going to marry you, and I had to tell you no. That was when the wall went up and you suddenly started looking at me as if you hated me.'

Face distant, she said, 'I was frank with you too, Liam. I'm sick of living alone; I want someone else there, someone to share things with, someone to come home to every day.'

'Was that the only reason you slept with me—to get me to marry you?'

She bristled, glaring at him. 'Don't be so insulting! I thought we had a real relationship; I thought you cared about me.'

'I do! That has nothing to do with getting married—' He broke off, staring at nothing, his brow corrugated, then muttered, 'Look, Kit, I gave you my reasons the other day. I asked you not to take my answer personally—'

Incredulously she interrupted, 'How else can I take it, for heaven's sake? You want me to sleep with you but you don't love me enough to marry me. I take that very personally.'

His voice rough, he said, 'I never wanted to hurt you, Kit. That's the last thing I want to do. Please believe that. This isn't about you, it's about me. I prefer to live alone; I don't want to live with anyone, not ever again.'

'Weren't you happy with Claudia?'

She had never once asked him about his dead wife or their relationship; she had realised early on that Liam did not want to talk about any of that. She had felt a door close in her face every time she'd mentioned Claudia.

Now there was a long silence, then Liam said tersely, 'I'm sorry, I can't discuss her with you of all people.'

She flinched at his tone—it was like a slap in the face. It pushed her away, denied her the right to ask him questions. This was why she felt so uneasy about their relationship. There were areas of his life that he would not talk about, and while he locked her out of his most private thoughts how could she really understand him, or feel she really knew him? What sort of man hid himself from someone he had known most of his life?

'What do you mean...me of all people?' she asked in pain.

He sighed, rubbing a hand across his temples as if he had a headache. 'Oh, for heaven's sake, Kit—isn't it obvious?'

'I've talked to you about Hugh; I don't keep secrets from you.'

'Hugh's alive. Claudia is dead. It wouldn't be fair to her.'

'How can you hurt her now she's dead? I'm alive too, Liam, and I need a man who cares enough about me to want to live with me, not just sleep with me now and then.'

His eyes flashed; she felt the violence seething behind his face and tensed.

At that second some new arrivals came through the door with a loud crash, chattering noisily; they paused to grin and nod to them, saying, 'Morning!' before settling down on the seats opposite to eat bacon sandwiches and drink tea.

Kit picked up her mug of coffee and drank some although it tasted bitter on her tongue; Liam grimly followed suit. They couldn't talk with people sitting there eavesdropping.

As they walked across the road back to the Victorian school house, the spring sunlight shifting through branches just breaking into leaf, Liam said tersely, 'So it's over, is it? Just like that? I won't marry you so you're dropping me in favour of what's-his-name?'

Kit hadn't meant that at all; she went white, her colour flooding from her face so suddenly that she felt icy cold, as if she was about to faint.

'I never said that!'

Liam wasn't looking at her; he was staring up at the cloudy March sky, his profile hard, stony. 'But that's the situation, isn't it? You gave me an ultimatum. Either I marry you or we stop seeing each other.'

'It wasn't an ultimatum!'

'Oh, for God's sake! Why are you arguing about semantics? We both know what you meant, don't we? If I don't want to marry you you won't sleep with me again.'

They had reached the door of the school. He looked down at her and Kit stared back, her face clenched in misery and anger.

'Yes, that's what I said,' she agreed. 'I want a man who loves me enough to want to live with me, a man who loves me enough to be ready to make a commitment to me in front of everyone we know and care about. Obviously that man isn't you. I thought it was; I'm sorry if I embarrassed you.'

She opened the door and walked into the hall without looking back so she had no idea how Liam took what she had said.

When she reached their stall she said to Paddy and Fred, 'Your turn to go and have coffee. I'll take over.'

Paddy looked at her in an odd way, her eyes worried. 'Are you feeling OK, Kit?'

'I'm fine,' she said offhandedly.

'Well, if you're sure,' Paddy said, not convinced, and let Fred lead her away, his arm around her.

Kit watched them go, envying them their close and warm relationship. There was no shadow on their love; she couldn't remember them ever quarrelling or even disagreeing about anything important. She sensed that their love was not intense; it had no ups and downs, no highs and lows; they were simply happy with each other. It must be marvellous, she thought.

She had never felt like that about Hugh, nor he about her. Their marriage had been happy enough in a quiet, uneventful, unimaginative way, but then she had never known anything different, so why would she have complained? She had thought all marriages were like that—a compromise, a calm, resigned acceptance of what life had handed you. When Hugh had suddenly fallen in love with someone else she had been startled rather than stricken. She had never blamed him for leaving her; she had simply been envious, wishing it would happen to her.

She had thought that she would never fall in love, that it was too late for her, that she had missed her chance by marrying Hugh for all the wrong reasons. It hadn't occurred to her that she might fall in love in the autumn of her life rather than the spring—and not with a chance-met stranger, the way Hugh had, but with someone she had known for years without ever remotely suspecting that he might one day come to mean the whole world to her.

She and Liam had known each other most of their adult lives, but for most of that time they had each been married—Kit to Hugh and Liam to Claudia, a beautiful but delicate, rather pale and listless woman who had died seven years ago. Kit knew that Liam had been stricken by her death; he must have been to have taken so long to recover from it.

She had seen very little of Claudia, and had rarely seen Liam with his wife, come to that. They had not entertained in their home very often and Claudia had had no interest in antiques; she had not collected anything and she had never shown up at the firm, not even to the Christmas party given for the staff every year.

Liam had almost never spoken about Claudia while she had been alive, and since her death he'd never mentioned her at all. Kit didn't like to ask probing questions—if he didn't want to talk about Claudia then that was OK with her—or at least it had been in the beginning, but increasingly his silence bothered her.

What were the secrets locked inside him? Had he been passionately in love with his wife? Was he still grieving for her? Hadn't he got over it at all? Why was he so secretive, so reluctant to talk about his feelings?

How could any relationship work with a man who refused to talk about himself? At one time Kit had believed that she knew him so well, but as the months had gone by she'd realised that she hardly knew him at all. She only knew what Liam wanted her to know. The rest was silence.

She knew his children, of course, and got on well with them. Liam had often brought them into the auction rooms when they were younger: they had gone to the same children's parties as Kit's son, and been at the same school. It had usually been Liam who'd taken them there in his car, dropping them off on his way to work.

He and Kit had seen each other often at school concerts and prize-givings. Hugh had always been too busy to go along to parent-teachers' associations or attend school functions. His work had occupied all his time—Kit had never known why Claudia had taken so little interest in her children's lives.

Liam and Claudia had had two children, both of whom were now married and living elsewhere: Geraldine, who was twenty-five, was living in Holland with her Dutch dentist husband and two-year-old daughter; Felix, his son, who was now twenty-seven, worked in advertising in London and lived in a flat by the river with his actress wife, Leila, and eighteen-month-old son, Gerald.

The Christmas before last there had been a family gathering in Liam's beautiful Georgian home when both Geraldine and Felix had stayed with their families for a week. Kit had spent Boxing Day with them.

She liked both of Liam's children, and they were always friendly towards her. She didn't think that they suspected the nature of her relationship with Liam, but at least neither Geraldine nor Felix resented her presence in their father's life.

No doubt, she thought with bitter humour, they knew how little she meant to him! They didn't fear her taking their mother's place. They were probably sure that Liam would never marry again. It was humiliating to imagine them asking Liam if he meant to marry her, and Liam assuring them that he never would.

No! He wouldn't talk about her with his children, any more than he would talk about his wife with her.

In any case, he saw his children very rarely. They kept in touch by phone, and visited at long intervals, but they all had busy, preoccupied lives and lived too far from their father to see much of him. If Liam resented that he never said anything, and he was certainly not lonely. He had a busy life himself, and many friends in this small, close-knit English town.

Kit saw rather more of her own son and his family because although they only made the trip back to

Silverburn once or twice a year Kit visited them
more often. Paul and Claire lived in Edinburgh,
which was a very enjoyable city to visit; Kit loved
going up there to stay in their comfortable, beautifully run home, spending time with her grand-
children, little Ian and his sister Kate, named
Katherine, for her, but given a different
abbreviation.

They were adorable, and Kit was always happy
to babysit them so that their parents could have an
evening out together. She was lucky to like her
daughter-in-law; Paul had chosen well. She and
Claire had got on from the start. They liked the
same things and shared the same attitudes.

Kit had been taken aback when Paul had got
married so young, just after leaving university, but
she had not attempted to argue him out of it—nor
shown any sign of disapproval, not because she
didn't care—in fact it had deepened her own sense
of loneliness after the divorce; she had felt she was
losing her son as well as her husband—but because
she had brought Paul up to be independent and
self-sufficient, and she liked his chosen wife and
respected his judgement, even if she was worried
about his decision.

It had been some time before she'd recognised
why Paul had acted the way he had. Oh, he loved
Claire and they were clearly very happy, but Paul
had rushed into marriage because he had been upset
when his father had left and their family life had
broken up. He had married early to re-establish a

family life around himself, give himself back his sense of security.

Talking to her daughter-in-law one day a year ago, Kit had discovered that Claire knew precisely why Paul had wanted to get married so soon. A warm, maternal girl with calm eyes, Claire had said frankly, 'I wanted to look after him; he was really hurt about his dad leaving. He needed me, and it made me happy to know that. It has worked out, Kit, don't worry.'

'I can see that,' she had said, smiling back at her.

But understanding why Paul had rushed into marriage hadn't helped her much. It had still hurt to realise that her son hadn't turned to her for comfort. She felt she had failed Paul.

'It must have been even tougher for you,' Claire had said that day, watching her, and Kit had given her a wry look.

'No, I wasn't broken up by the divorce—my marriage hadn't been a good one for years and I understood why Hugh left. Funnily enough, we get on better now than we ever did before. We've become friends, and I like Tina; she's a nice girl. I think Paul was much more upset than I was; it was a shock to him, but it wasn't to me.'

But, although it hadn't hurt her, she had felt rather at sea for a while. At one fell swoop she had lost both husband and son; the landscape of her life had changed overnight. It had been Liam who had helped her to rebuild her life, encouraged her to take up new interests, make new friends.

She had gone to art classes and learnt to paint; she had gone to evening class to learn Spanish and then Italian; she had done a course in cordon bleu cookery. For several years she had filled her time with feverish activity, but slowly she had begun to get over her loneliness and sense of failure.

Liam had been a godsend. She had known him and his wife for years before she had begun working with him after Claudia's death. When Kit and Hugh had got divorced they'd sold their beautiful and valuable Victorian home, and in their amicable divorce settlement they'd shared fifty-fifty the money raised by the sale of the house and its contents.

Each of them had kept their favourite pieces of furniture and some of the antiques that they had jointly owned; the rest had all been sold and had raised a considerable amount.

Kit had bought her flat in a new block in Townwall Street, right in the centre of town, and the rest of her money had then been invested in Liam's firm, after which, at Liam's suggestion, she'd become a partner. By then her whole life had begun to revolve around the auction rooms and Liam.

Ah, but when did I fall in love with him? she thought now.

It had not been a sudden lightning blow—more of a slow growth, subterranean, unadmitted, secret. One day she had simply woken up and realised how she felt about him, and the realisation had been a shock, especially as she couldn't believe that Liam would ever feel the same about her.

The first time he'd kissed her had been the Christmas before last, under the mistletoe at a party at a friend's house. He had looked up and seen the white berries and green leaves pinned on the chandelier above them, and had given her a quick, amused glance.

'We can't waste this opportunity, can we?' he'd said, and then his mouth had come down and found hers.

Passion had hit her like a tidal wave; feeling had poured through her and left her weak at the knees, clutching at him for support.

He had lifted his head, his eyes half-veiled by his lids, and had said huskily, 'I should have done that long ago.'

He had walked her home later, and she had invited him in for a hot drink on that icy December night. They had both known that he was not leaving; he had stayed until morning and her whole world had looked different the next day. She could remember her happiness with incredulity now. She had known that she was in love, had believed that Liam felt the same.

That was how it had started.

Now it was over. Just as suddenly and without warning. And Kit knew that she would never get over losing him.

'Hello again!'

She started at the voice and looked up in disbelief. Joe Ingram was standing in front of the stall.

'What are you doing here?' Kit asked, and he gave her that charming, lazy grin.

'I went along to your auction rooms and found a nice little girl typing and answering the phone. She told me I'd find you here.'

'Cherie!' Kit revealed. Their secretary had only been with them a few months; she had come to the firm straight from school. Pretty, cheerful, lively, she was an asset to the firm; everybody liked her.

'Is that her name?' Joe laughed, his head thrown back, and she sensed the other stallholders staring at them, especially the women.

'She pronounces it Cherry, actually,' Kit said, smiling at him. 'But it is spelt Cherie. Her parents had a honeymoon in Paris and wanted to give her a French name.'

'It suits her; she's very cute.'

'Very,' agreed Kit drily. 'But she shouldn't have told you where to find me; she's supposed to be more discreet than that.'

'Oh, don't tell her off! It wasn't her fault—I told her I was a friend of yours.'

'I'm working!'

Joe picked up a nineteenth-century German piece—a boy in blue jacket and white breeches, a gun across his arm, a tan and white spaniel close to his heels.

'Eighty pounds,' Kit told him before he looked at the price.

He made a face. 'A bit steep, but I'll have it,' he said, and wrote out a cheque at once. As he held it out to her he asked, 'I see they do lunch across the road at a pub. Is it any good?'

'Very good. Today's special is rabbit casserole, and that's something they always do well.' Kit began wrapping the little boy and his spaniel in tissue paper; she slid the parcel into a plastic carrier bag and held it out to Joe.

Taking it, he said, 'Sounds delicious; I love rabbit—will you have lunch with me?'

Kit hesitated, conscious of Paddy and Fred a few feet away and undoubtedly listening. They knew that she had been seeing Liam for months—they would be eaten up with surprise and curiosity if she accepted.

Then, across the room, she met Liam's cold, hostile eyes. He was back talking to the pre-Raphaelite with the soft, twisting red curls. I might have known he would be with her! Kit thought bitterly. Making arrangements to see her for dinner tonight, no doubt. Yet he glares at me in that dog-in-the-manger way! He won't live with me, yet he wants to own me! Well, he doesn't, and what's sauce for the goose is sauce for the gander.

Bristling, she looked back at Joe. 'OK—I'll have to have an early lunch, though. I'll see you over in the pub at twelve-thirty?'

'Twelve-thirty across the road,' he agreed, his eyes bright, and she felt a qualm of guilt. It wasn't fair to him to use him in her war with Liam; she wouldn't want to lead him on, give him the wrong idea.

But he had already turned and was walking away. She stared after him, biting her lip uncertainly. Should she call him back, cancel their appointment?

But having lunch with the man wasn't a big commitment, was it? She would meet him in the pub and eat a quick lunch. There was no reason why she shouldn't be friendly to him—but she wouldn't accept any more invitations.

Even to annoy Liam.

CHAPTER THREE

THEY had a busy morning after that; Kit sold a number of smaller items and one or two really valuable pieces, and was kept so occupied that there was no chance, luckily, for Liam to talk to her although he had come back to the stall a few seconds after Joe had left. She had had the feeling that he had hurried to get over here to meet Joe, but he had been just too late.

After that she had frequently felt Liam watching her, and when she told Paddy very casually to take over on the stall because she was going to lunch now, she was meeting someone she sensed his head swing round. The hairs on the back of her neck stood up at the fixed stare directed at her carefully averted profile. He was too busy making a sale to be able to speak to her, though; she had chosen her moment carefully, and she pretended not to have noticed his look.

Paddy had heard Joe invite her to lunch and was consumed with curiosity. 'Right,' she said, taking a quick look at Liam to see his reaction and then hurriedly looking away again as she met the glacial pierce of his stare. 'We'll go to lunch when you get back, then. I'll be quite glad about that; we had such a big, late breakfast. Fred ate the full works—eggs, bacon, sausage, toast and marmalade—the lot! I don't know how he manages to eat so much and stay so slim; he must have hollow legs.'

Kit glanced across the room—Fred was carrying a red-velvet-upholstered Victorian buttonback chair through the crowded hall, out to the car of the woman who had just bought it. Kit had tried picking it up a few minutes ago; it was made of oak and very heavy, but Fred carried it as if it were a toy.

'Oh, but Fred works so hard, he burns up every calorie he eats.'

Paddy looked indulgently across the room, smiling. 'Yes, he does, that's true.'

Kit picked up her handbag from under the counter. 'Well, I'll be off, then.'

She began to walk very fast because Liam was still occupied with his customer and couldn't stop her, but she was still nervous—would he follow her across to the pub?

What was the matter with the man? He wanted everything his own way, wanted to have his cake and eat it, and was sulky and brooding if she refused to let him dictate what happened. Typical man, in fact! she thought bitterly. Weren't they all the same? Well, Liam wasn't getting his own way this time.

All the same, she had had enough confrontation for one morning; she didn't want another row with him, or to have him deliberately picking some sort of quarrel with Joe—something he was quite capable of.

She felt his gaze fixed on her back like a knife right between her shoulderblades, and shivered—but she didn't look back or hesitate, her slender body in the smooth coffee silk moving purposefully out of the hall. Damn him! He was about to get a lesson in life in the real world. She was not putting up with any more from him.

Joe was already in the pub waiting for her, a glass of lager in front of him as he studied the menu written up in chalk on a blackboard displayed on the wall. The bar was already crowded; voices rose on all sides as she walked across the room.

He rose, his face breaking into an immediate smile. 'You've come!'

'I said I would,' she said, sitting down beside him on the red plush seat.

'I was afraid you'd change your mind. What will you have to drink?'

'A glass of white wine, please—and I'm going to have rabbit casserole.'

'Same here; I'll order it now, then.' He went up to the bar and she watched the barmaid—a small, skinny girl in a neat navy blue apron that was far too big for her—going pink and laughing as Joe chatted her up and ordered their meals.

He really is a charmer! But if he turns that charm on every woman he meets his apparent interest in you really doesn't mean much, Kit thought wryly.

He came back with her glass of white wine and sat down, turning to her with a smile. His blue eyes turned serious, assessing her expression.

'What's wrong?'

'Nothing.' She picked up her wine. 'Thank you for this.'

'My pleasure,' he murmured, still watching her. 'Come on, what's going on inside that head of yours? I know something is wrong so don't lie.'

She looked into the golden liquid in her glass, her silvery hair falling smoothly against her cheek. 'Oh, it's just that I'm not sure I should be here. I don't really want to get involved, or waste your time.'

'I don't see having a pleasant lunch with you as a waste of my time!'

She looked at him through her darkened lashes. 'So long as you understand that that's all there is to it.'

His blue eyes glinted with humour. 'I'm not expecting to buy you with one pub lunch!'

She went faintly pink and laughed. 'Of course not—but you know what I mean! I told you—'

'That there's someone else in your life. I know. Was he the slightly glowering character I saw working on your stall this morning?'

She was taken aback. He was very observant. 'That's my partner, Liam Keble,' she murmured, then laughed. 'The description is very accurate, though.' Not that Liam would have been amused by it—not in his present mood, anyway!

'Oh, I know who he is; I asked someone about him and they told me it was Liam Keble, the local auctioneer. I wasn't sure whether or not he was the mystery man in your life, though. I'd seen him with someone else earlier, and I'd got the impression he was very interested in *her*.'

She was conscious of him watching her intently and hid the stab of pain she felt, looking away, fighting to keep a calm expression on her face. So he had noticed that Liam was interested in that sleek little redhead? That was who Joe meant, she was sure of that. But she didn't want to betray her jealousy to him, or anyone. Especially Liam.

Joe waited and when she didn't answer asked quietly, 'Is she the reason why you went out alone last night? Did he dump you for her?'

She flashed him an angry, green-eyed stare. 'I didn't say I'd been dumped!'

'You aren't rapturously happy, though, are you?'

He was too shrewd. 'Can we drop this subject? I don't want to talk about my private life.'

He was silent for a moment then said in a low voice, 'I didn't mean to upset you. I'm sorry.'

She sighed. 'Look, we only met last night—you may talk to strangers at the drop of a hat but I'm just a small-town girl; I wasn't brought up to do that.'

'Maybe it's time you learnt not to be so buttoned up?'

'And maybe it's time you learnt to mind your own business!' Her voice had risen and people at the other tables were glancing round at them, whispering to each other. Kit's colour went up too and she was tempted to walk out of there, but at that moment the barmaid arrived with their plates of rabbit casserole. As she put them on the table she gave Joe a flirtatious look.

'I brought it to you myself, see?'

His frown had vanished like snow in June. He gave the girl another of those charming smiles. 'I'm honoured!'

'You should be! I don't do that for everyone!' The barmaid gave Kit a quick, assessing glance that took in her silvered hair, the faint lines around her eyes and mouth. She smiled—old enough to be her mother, was undoubtedly her conclusion!

Looking back at Joe, the girl said, 'Well, if you want anything else let me know,' fluttering her thick clusters of eyelashes at him in a meaningful way.

Joe laughed and Kit couldn't help laughing too, a little wryly, envying her that ability to be so direct. She obviously fancied Joe and wanted him to know that she did. Kit had never been that blunt or open.

'You dangerous woman!' Joe said, and the barmaid giggled.

'You can talk!' she said, then looked at Kit. 'He's a flirt, isn't he?'

'A terrible flirt,' Kit agreed drily.

'But cute with it!'

'If you like the type,' said Kit.

'Hey, do you two mind not talking about me as if I wasn't here?' he demanded.

'Oh, did we hurt its little feelings, then?' the barmaid cooed at him mockingly.

From behind the bar the landlady called out to her. 'Are you working here, Bella, or just chatting to the customers? People are waiting to order drinks!'

'Coming,' the barmaid called, and gave a sigh. 'No peace for the wicked! Enjoy your rabbit casserole.' She leaned over and patted Joe's cheek. 'Diddums!'

'Be careful—I might bite!' he said, eyes twinkling.

'Ooh, promises, promises,' she said, then fled.

Joe met Kit's wry gaze. He grimaced. 'Sorry, a habit of years—flirting with waitresses and barmaids. When you live alone and travel the world year in, year out you talk to any friendly face you see.'

'Especially if it's female!'

Unabashed, he laughed. 'OK, that's true, but not just any women. Lonely men hit on barmaids because they get paid to be nice to customers and don't expect you to follow it up by asking them out. You just spend a cheerful hour or so with them and both enjoy the chat and the fun. If they didn't like that sort of thing most girls wouldn't work in bars.'

'Hmm,' she said, unconvinced.

He watched her face, his mouth crooked. 'You're a tough lady, do you know that? Shall we eat our food before it gets cold?'

It was good, the rabbit perfectly cooked in a liquid which had a pale golden colour and was delicately flavoured with herbs; there were tiny herb dumplings, and vegetables which were still firm but tender—carrot and onion, red and green peppers, green beans, and creamed potatoes. They had also been brought a separate dish of pickled red cabbage.

'Fabulous,' Joe said, finishing with a sigh of satisfaction. 'I must eat here again. How often is there an antiques fair in the village school?'

'Once a month.'

'There were so many stalls as well! There must be dozens of antiques shops in this area.'

'Oh, the dealers come from all over this part of the country, not just from Silverburn.'

The landlady herself came over to collect their plates and ask if they wanted a dessert or just coffee to follow. They elected to have coffee and it arrived a moment later.

'This is good too,' Joe said, drinking some. 'Good, strong coffee. I'm really impressed with this place. Do they do dinner too?'

'Yes, of course.'

'Well, made up your mind yet?' he asked and Kit looked at him blankly, bewildered by the question.

'What are you talking about?'

'Me. Do you trust me enough now to have dinner with me?'

'I just had lunch with you! I'm not ready to have dinner with you too.'

'How about breakfast, then?'

Her green eyes flashed. 'I don't think that's funny!' She picked up her cup, finished her coffee and got up. 'I must get back.'

She was outside the pub before Joe caught up with her. He took hold of her arm, halting her midstep, and Kit gave him a furious look.

'Do you mind? Let go of me!'

'You have a very nasty temper,' he complained. 'I was just being funny—I didn't mean what you thought I meant.'

'I should hope not!' she snapped. 'Whether you did or not I still have to get back to work.'

Pulling herself free, she walked across the road to the school. Before she went through the gate Joe suddenly pounced, his hands closing on her slim waist. Her feet left the ground; she gasped, grabbing for him; a second later she found herself perched like a bird on the top of the red-brick schoolyard wall, her legs dangling like a child's, staring down into Joe's teasing face.

'What do you think you're doing?' she asked breathlessly, but his expression was too disarming for her to stay angry and she began to laugh. 'You idiot! Get me down!' She would have jumped but the wall was just too high for it to be a safe thing to do.

'Not until you've said you believe me! And anyway, you look about five stuck up there; it suits you!'

Highly flushed, she snapped at him, 'Help me down!'

'In a minute.' He touched her delicate, dark chocolate-coloured leather high heels with one finger. 'What pretty shoes—and pretty feet inside them, too. I've never seen such tiny feet; they're like a doll's; what size are they, for heaven's sake?'

She kicked one at him furiously and he jumped back. A second later behind her she heard the door of the school opening with a creak. 'Get me down before someone sees me!' she hissed.

'Do you believe I was only joking about having breakfast with me?' Joe insisted.

'Yes, yes—get me down!' She looked over her shoulder and her heart nearly stopped in horror. Oh, no! It would be him, wouldn't it?

Liam was standing a few feet away. His grey eyes were as cold as charity; she shivered as she met them briefly before looking away.

Beside him stood the redhead she had seen him talking to earlier; she was staring at Kit too, but she was smiling, and Kit hated her.

'Get me down!' Kit told Joe through her teeth, and he looked past her at the newcomers, his blue eyes narrowing in comprehension.

He lifted her down just as the redhead came out of the gate and gave Joe a flick of her long lashes and that cat-like, triangular, curling smile. 'Having fun?'

He promptly asked her, 'Want to play? Shall I put you up there?'

'No, thank you!' The other woman backed, afraid that he might do so anyway.

'Cowardy custard!'

Joe's flirting again, Kit thought without jealousy, far more aware of Liam's angry, insistent eyes and carefully avoiding looking in his direction.

'You'd ruin my skirt!' the redhead told Joe, who looked down at the pencil-slim black skirt.

'Oh, I'd certainly hate to do that.' He glanced sideways at Kit's elegant coffee-coloured silk dress.

'Kit, I didn't ruin your dress, did I?' He took a step backwards to look at the back of her skirt, then brushed the material with his hand, his touch lingering a few seconds on the warm curve of her behind.

'OK, just a touch of brick dust; it's gone now, no harm done!'

Kit knew she had flushed, mostly because she had felt the leap of rage in Liam at seeing that intimate contact, brief though it had been.

'You should be back at work, not playing stupid games out here!' His voice was like a whiplash; Kit looked at him furiously. How dared he talk to her in that tone in front of other people?

Joe's brows met as if the tone annoyed him too, but he sounded polite enough. 'Introduce us, Kit.'

Through stiff lips she muttered, 'This is my partner, Liam Keble. Liam, this is Joe Ingram.'

Joe moved as if to offer his hand, then met Liam's piercing eyes and thought better of it, his brows rising in silent comment on that glare. He nodded instead.

'Hi.'

Liam nodded back, even more curtly. 'You're the war photographer, aren't you? I hope you aren't under the impression that this might turn into a war zone before long.'

Joe laughed. 'The last thing I want is to see another war, thanks.' He looked at the redhead standing beside Liam. 'I'm looking for peace and quiet. What do you think my chances are of finding it?' he asked her, and she laughed.

'It depends on the company you keep, I imagine!'
What did that mean? thought Kit.

The other woman looked at her as if reading her
expression. 'You're Kit Randall, aren't you? Liam's
been telling me about you.'

Oh, had he? Kit thought resentfully. What exactly
had he been saying? She didn't want him telling
this woman anything about her. But she reluctantly
took the hand offered and forced a smile.

'How do you do?' Her tone was polite but cool,
and she saw that register in the other woman's
strange, yellowish eyes. Kit had seen eyes like that
on tigers in the zoo and had been glad that there'd
been strong bars between them and her. She felt
like that now.

All the same the other woman went on smiling,
although her smile had chilled a little. 'I'm Cary
Burnaby—I think you knew my uncle, Steven
Burnaby? I've inherited his business, so I expect
we'll be running into each other again from time
to time. I'll probably be visiting the auction rooms
soon to look for new stock.'

Kit stared at her, not seeing any resemblance to
Steven, who had been a very short, rather ugly old
man with white hair and a goatee. He had had a
shop near the church—a bay-windowed, gabled old
building from the seventeenth century, with ancient
tiling and chimneys which looked as if any strong
wind might blow them down.

Steven had both sold antique clocks and repaired
them. In his seventies, with the tiny, delicate fingers
of a clockmaker, and rather myopic eyes behind

pebbly glasses, he had known more about clocks than anyone Kit had ever met, and she had been very sorry to hear of his death during the coldest month of the winter.

'I was very fond of Steven,' Kit said. 'He taught me a lot about clocks and I was shocked to hear of his death—I miss him.'

Cary Burnaby assessed her again. 'That's nice. I'm sure he'd be pleased if he could hear you.' The words were warm, but the voice in which they were delivered was not—Cary Burnaby had a cool, clear voice, with a silvery note like the chime of a clock.

She gestured with one hand, and Kit noted that she had very similar fingers to Steven. That much they certainly had in common—those small, delicate hands which were essential for the fine working parts of a watch or clock. Cary, however, varnished them in clear, pale varnish and had whitened the ends of each nail in the French style.

'Yes, he taught me a lot too. When I was at school we used to come down and visit him for a few weeks every summer, and I spent hours every day hanging around the shop, listening to him. I suppose that's why he left it to me, but then, there was nobody else. Steven never married; I was his only close relative. My father was his half-brother and much younger, although he died first. I don't think Steven had many friends, either. He had a lot of acquaintances, mostly in the business, but very few people visited him at home.'

'He always seemed very lonely,' agreed Kit with sympathy for the dead man.

'Well, he was really only interested in his clocks; they took the place of a family for Steven,' shrugged Cary Burnaby. 'I won't make that mistake!'

'Have you had any training apart from learning from your uncle in the school holidays?' Kit was rather dubious about someone taking over so specialised a business without a long apprenticeship.

'Oh, yes; I worked for three years for a London clockmaker and after that I worked in the V&A and learned a lot more.'

Kit was impressed; she had often visited the Victoria and Albert Museum to see their wonderful collection of ceramics and she knew how difficult it was to get a job with them.

'Steven must have been very proud of you,' she murmured, and Cary gave her a genuine smile for the first time, her yellow eyes lighting up.

'I think he was, yes.' She glanced sideways at Liam's taut profile and blinked, only then taking in his grim mood. 'Well, we'd better get to lunch; it was nice talking to you,' she said to Kit, and then turned her smile on Liam. 'Sorry to hold you up— shall we go?'

He nodded, and stalked away with Cary hurrying along beside him on very high black heels. He hadn't even looked at Kit again.

She turned rather blindly towards the school-hall door and heard Joe say softly, 'I'll be on my way, then. May I ring you in a day or so? If you won't have dinner with me, how about going fishing at the weekend?'

'Fishing?' she repeated, not really listening.

'Yes, I'm a keen fisherman—it's a quiet, peaceful way of spending a day; we could take a picnic and eat on the river bank.'

'You're obsessed with eating!'

He laughed, then persisted, 'Will you come? Sunday? I'll bring the picnic.'

'It sounds a dull way of spending a Sunday,' she grumbled. 'And I'm not sure I approve of fishing.'

'It's a trout river, and you said you liked trout.'

'Did I? When?'

'In the pub.'

'Oh. What a memory!'

Softly he said, 'Please come Kit. You'll enjoy it, I'm sure you will; it's very restful sitting on the river bank on a quiet spring morning, listening to the water and the birds.'

It was tempting, the way he described it—although she had a strong suspicion that it would turn out to be very uncomfortable, especially if it rained, as it well might. March was not the warmest of months or the driest. On the other hand, if she wasn't seeing Liam any more she would have a lot of free time on her hands.

'OK,' she said. 'What time?'

'Eight o'clock?'

'In the morning?'

He laughed at her horrified voice. 'You have to get up early to fish.'

'I thought that was birds, catching worms?'

'And fish,' he assured her. 'Lots of people will get there much earlier—before dawn, some of them.

It's the light, you see—you make less shadow on the water.'

'Well, I'm not doing any fishing! I'll just watch you.'

'OK, see you Sunday, eight o'clock.' He leaned over and kissed her lightly on the cheek before she knew what he meant to do. It was a warm brush of his mouth and her eyes opened wide in surprise.

The next second he had gone, walking rapidly towards his car, parked along the road. Kit stared after him, still feeling that touch of his mouth on her skin. It was an odd sensation—like a teenager's first kiss, innocent and sweet. She carried it with her when she went back to work.

When Liam got back from lunch she was humming under her breath as she wrapped a knife box and a set of silver-plated fish knives and forks for a customer who was coming back for them in half an hour.

He gave her a sharp look, eyes cold and narrowed. 'Whistling while you work? You look very pleased with yourself.'

The knife-edged tone made her stop humming; she gave him a cool stare. 'Why shouldn't I be?'

His mouth curled cynically. 'Oh, no reason—if you don't mind being a laughing stock that's up to you. Everyone saw you with Ingram and they're all gossiping away like mad. I told you it would raise eyebrows if you went out with a man ten years younger than you.'

Fizzing with outrage, she flung back at him, 'They can mind their own business—and so can you!'

He snapped right back. 'It is my business. You're my partner. I don't want a scandal involving the firm.'

'Scandal? What are you talking about? Don't be so ridiculous. Joe's free and so am I.'

Their eyes met; she saw the smouldering rage in his and tensed, her pulse beating like a drum. Liam was angrier than she had ever seen him; she waited for him to say something, to deny it, to say, No, you're not free, you belong to me; don't go, Kit, I don't want to lose you.

The silence lengthened and she knew he wasn't going to; he wouldn't try to persuade her to stay with him. Either his pride wouldn't let him or he was simply angry because she had found someone else.

Her heart slowed down again to a heavy, depressing beat; she felt cold and on the point of tears. Then she got angry too. What on earth did he want? That she should accept their relationship obediently on his terms without question? That she should stay faithful to him although he wasn't prepared to alter his life in any way for her?

But he certainly didn't intend to be faithful to her—after all, he'd asked Cary Burnaby to dinner before he'd seen her with Joe!

With a jagged shock she wondered if he ever had been faithful to her. Had there been other women all along? That had never occurred to her before.

If anyone had suggested it a few months ago she wouldn't even have listened; she would have been furious, would have laughed at the idea.

But that was before it had begun to dawn on her how one-sided her relationship with Liam was—how selfish he was! He wanted her in his bed, but he wouldn't give up anything for her, or share with her, or let the world see that they belonged together.

He wanted to be free. But not her. Oh, no, he did not like the idea of her being free at all.

Well, it was time he realised that he couldn't have things his own way.

'I'm as free as the birds, Liam,' she said bleakly, and he turned on his heel and walked away without saying another word.

CHAPTER FOUR

OVER the next few days the gulf between them widened all the time. Kit felt as if she was on one ice-floe and Liam on another, drifting fast in opposite directions. He rarely spoke to her; if he was forced to he used a curt, offhand tone that made her hackles rise. His face was grim, his grey eyes were flints that occasionally struck sparks of fire when they looked at her.

She avoided him as much as she could, but it wasn't easy when you were partners in a busy firm. When they were in the same room she fought to make herself look calm and unruffled, but Liam's temper was on a short fuse and so was her own. If anyone else was around they managed some sort of polite pretence, but if they were alone it wasn't long before they exploded into fierce argument, yelling each other down, or else Liam would turn on his heel and stalk off with a face like thunder.

Paddy and Fred looked bewildered and worried as the days went by and the atmosphere between them grew worse. Paddy often seemed about to say something, but whenever she opened her mouth to start Kit gave her a warning glance and she sighed and fell silent.

Kit did not want to talk about what was going on. In any case, what was there to say? When you had split up with someone, nobody else could do anything about it, and there was no point in talking about it, except to find comfort, and she did not want comfort from anybody. She felt like somebody who had suffered a serious burn—her skin was far too tender to be touched even by the lightest and most gentle fingers.

She knew that he was seeing Cary Burnaby, who rang up several times that week. Kit took one of the calls. She and Liam were working on a catalogue for an auction when the phone rang; Kit picked it up, and heard the silvery chime of Cary's voice.

'Could I speak to Liam, please?'

'Yes, he's here.' Kit held the phone out to him, avoiding his eyes. 'For you—Cary Burnaby.'

'Hi, Cary,' he said into the phone, sounding warm and intimate, and Kit's whole body clenched in a wave of jealousy.

She walked away and poured herself another cup of coffee from a pot which Paddy had just brought them. Drinking it, she stood by the window, staring out over the townscape of roofs, chimneys, church spires and, beyond that, the woods and fields around Silverburn. Pigeons waddled along the window-ledge, soft dove-grey, like the sky on this cool March day.

Kit tried to think about something else, fought not to listen to Liam talking, laughing, but couldn't help it; even though his voice was low she could hear every word.

'I'm glad you enjoyed it. Yes, the food is very good there, isn't it? I told you they did duck very well—and my sole was perfectly cooked.'

Kit knew where they had eaten dinner; Liam had often taken her there, and she had eaten the duck with cherries which was one of the restaurant's specialties. How could he take her there? It's our place, she thought, watching the pigeons flutter up into the sky.

'I'd love to have dinner at your place,' Liam said from behind her, and Kit stared fixedly at the roofs across the way. So she's cooking for him now! she thought.

I bet she's a terrific cook, too. Cordon bleu. She looks the type to be brilliant at anything she does. If she isn't brilliant at something, she doesn't do it. She won't be second-rate or simply mediocre; she has to be the best, to shine, to be admired. Kit thought of those yellow, leonine eyes. Cary Burnaby was a predator; she might be lovely, but she had sharp claws and dangerous teeth.

'What time shall I get there? Seven? Can I bring a bottle of wine? We're eating fish? A white, then? I'll find something drinkable. OK, see you on Saturday, then.'

He hung up. Kit turned and walked back across the room to the desk where they had been working. She sat down with her coffee, ignoring his gaze.

'Where were we? Oh, yes—page nine, the set of Victorian dining-room chairs.'

* * *

That Saturday they worked in the morning until lunchtime. Liam came into Kit's little office and said offhandedly, 'I'm off now. Lock up, will you?'

She nodded, giving him the merest glance before looking back at the book she was consulting, checking the provenance of a piece of Meissen they had just been asked to put into their auction.

'Have a good weekend,' he said in a curt voice that made it sound like an insult.

'And you,' she said in the same sort of tone. She hoped he'd choke on whatever Cary Burnaby cooked for dinner that night.

Liam left, slamming the door on his way out. She glared at it, hating him.

Normally on Sunday Kit stayed in bed late, had a leisurely breakfast, and over the past fifteen months had usually spent the rest of the day with Liam, perhaps driving up to London to have lunch in one of their favourite restaurants and afterwards visiting a museum or art gallery before driving back to Silverburn.

If they hadn't gone to London Kit would sometimes cook their lunch and then they would curl up together on a sofa in her flat and read the Sunday papers or a book by the fire, listen to a favourite record, or watch TV, or just talk.

Those had been blissful weekends and her world without Liam was colder and paler. Kit felt an intense loneliness when she walked back into her flat that afternoon, knowing that she would not see Liam again until Monday.

The flat echoed with memories of their time together. Physical reminders of him were everywhere—a bottle of his aftershave in her bathroom cupboard, his short black towelling bathrobe hanging on the back of the bathroom door, a pair of pyjamas in a drawer in her bedroom, photos of them on tables and mantelshelves, compact discs they had bought together stacked beside her music centre, books of his on her bookshelves.

In a fit of depression that Saturday night she rushed about collecting up anything of Liam's she could find and putting it all into a cardboard box which she hid out of sight at the back of her wardrobe, but then her flat seemed horribly empty and bare, and her gloomy mood merely deepened.

She found it hard to get to sleep. She couldn't stop thinking about Liam having dinner with Cary Burnaby—was that all she had offered? Had Liam gone home or stayed the night?

She finally fell asleep towards the middle of the night, and when her alarm went off she found it even harder to wake up. She was tempted to stay in bed instead of getting up to meet Joe. The morning was grey and cool, and her bed was warm and cosy. She snuggled down under the duvet, yawning—why should she get up just to sit about on a cold river bank watching Joe fishing? Much more comfortable to stay where she was.

The only problem was that now she was wide awake her inconvenient mind at once came up with images of Liam—with Cary, with herself, memories that made her body wince, a knife twisting inside her until she was on the point of tears.

Oh, shut up! Forget him! she told herself, and, flinging back the duvet, she got out of bed and went into the bathroom. Ten minutes later she was dressed and ready, in old blue jeans and a checked shirt over which she wore a warm Fair Isle pullover with a well-washed beige background and softly fading multicoloured pattern.

She had knitted it herself for Hugh years ago, and he had left it behind when he'd moved out, and had told her to give it to a church jumble sale, but Kit kept forgetting to do that. She didn't often wear it, but it was very thick and comforting to wear on really cold days if you weren't too bothered about being seen wearing a man's sweater that was about three sizes too big for you!

She tied her silvery hair back from her face with a scrunchy hair band made of black velvet, put on a light make-up, and then had a quick breakfast— freshly squeezed orange juice, a slice of wholemeal toast and marmalade, coffee—while she glanced over the front page of the Sunday paper which had been pushed through her letter box as usual.

Joe arrived exactly on time just as she finished her toast. She might have known that he was the punctual type!

'Come in and have some coffee,' she invited, wanting another cup herself, but he shook his head.

'We're missing the best of the light—I'd rather go if you're ready.'

She saw his blue eyes wandering down over her sweater and jeans, and asked uncertainly, 'Is this suitable gear for fishing?' She hadn't known for sure what to put on.

'Perfect,' he nodded, then smiled. 'And I love the hairstyle—that and the baggy sweater make you look fifteen!'

She went faintly pink. 'I wish!'

'I don't,' he told her drily. 'I'd get arrested for what I'm thinking if you were!'

'Joe!' Her colour turned deep rose and he laughed at her.

'Anyway, I'm not into little girls—never was; I've always like older women.'

'Mother complex,' she muttered.

'Sad, isn't it?' he said, tongue-in-cheek. 'The only thing wrong is that those shoes won't do. You'll need boots—it will be muddy on the river bank. And put on a lined anorak with a hood if you've got one, just in case it rains.'

'I've got one,' she agreed. 'A waxed jacket with a hood—that should keep rain out unless we get a real downpour. But can you give me five minutes to get ready? I've only just finished breakfast.'

'OK,' he conceded rather reluctantly. 'I've already brought my car up from the car park; it's parked outside the main entrance, so come down when you're ready, but please hurry, Kit.'

'I will,' she promised, closing the door as he walked off.

She poured the rest of her pot of coffee into a vacuum flask, found two small cups and put them and her newspaper and a paperback thriller into a bag, then put on her racing-green anorak and dark green boots, found a small umbrella, checked her reflection in the hall mirror, and left the flat.

Joe watched her walk towards his car, leaned over, opened the passenger door and said, 'Love the boots; they should keep your feet dry even if the heavens open!'

'If it rains I'm not staying around long enough to get my feet wet anyway!' she assured him, getting into the seat beside him.

'You're over-civilised,' he said drily, shaking his head. 'It's time you got in touch with your natural self. Human beings are animals; they are made to survive in all kinds of weather, not skulk about indoors, avoiding contact with nature. What do you think Stone Age man did?'

'Hid at the back of his cave when it rained or snowed, if he had any sense.'

'If he had a woman like you around, you mean! So if it rains you'll desert me, will you? Then I'll eat your share of the picnic I've brought.'

In fact it didn't rain, although from time to time clouds drifted overhead through the soft grey sky. There wasn't much sunshine, although the sun did occasionally shine through the clouds; there was no wind, but it wasn't cold and there were quite a few people fishing along the river, some of them wading out into the tall, whispering reeds to cast their lines far out into the dimpled flow of water.

'Perfect fishing weather,' Joe said happily, drinking some of Kit's coffee. 'Are you enjoying yourself?'

She was leaning back in a canvas chair which Joe had dug out of his capacious car boot along with a large umbrella which fitted on to the back of the chair. She was as warm as toast in her jeans and anorak; she'd enjoyed her cup of coffee more than usual in the open air, and was slowly reading her way through her newspaper in between listening to the water lapping the sides of the bank, the cry of birds, the rustle of leaves.

'I think I am,' she said slowly, and Joe laughed.

'Don't sound so surprised!'

'I didn't think I would enjoy it.' She had always been far more inclined to stay indoors than spend her spare time in the open air.

'I know,' he said. 'But I told you you would.' His blue eyes sparkled and she gave him an amused, wry look.

'Don't sound so smug! If there's one thing I hate it's a smug man.'

He grinned at her, washing out his coffee-cup with a little water from a bottle of still mineral water he had brought with him. He dried it with a piece of paper towel, which he then carefully tucked back into a garbage bag to take back home, to dispose of later.

'I'm not smug; I'm just glad I was right about you. It means I'm really beginning to know you.'

She had no answer to that.

Sitting down again beside her, Joe murmured, 'Is it fun being a granny? That's something I really miss—not having had a child. I would have loved one.'

She gave him a sympathetic glance, smiling. 'It's not too late, Joe; you're only forty-two. Women reach the end of child-bearing in middle life but men don't. Men can go on having kids into old age if they have a younger wife. Find yourself a wife of child-bearing age and start a family.'

'That's too clinical for me. I'm not marrying just to have kids. If I get married it will be because I've fallen in love, and age will have nothing to do with it. I'd rather do without a family but have the experience of being in love.'

'You're a romantic!'

'I thought you realised that. Why do you think I was at that showing of *Camille*?' He stretched out, yawning and looking up at the sky which had turned a soft lavender colour and was streaked with primrose light.

'Looks as if the sun will be coming through by the afternoon. I do love English skies; they're always changing; the light's so soft and gentle. When you've lived abroad a lot in hot climates where the colours can knock your eyes out you start to long for the rain-washed greens and greys of English landscapes.'

Kit turned sideways to watch him thoughtfully. 'And I bet you've been through a very cynical phase, too, on your travels?'

He glanced at her, mouth crooked. 'Very shrewd. Yes, you're right. If you spend too much time in countries where corruption is rife and life is cheap you start to think anyone can be bought; you don't believe in anything or anybody. That's another reason why I dropped out of the life I was leading. I was sick of it all. Don't get me wrong; I'm not expecting life in a small English town to be perfect. I know you find corruption everywhere. I'm just looking for—' He broke off, shrugging. 'I don't know.'

'Your past?' suggested Kit softly. 'You told me you used to come here when you were a child. Maybe you remember those days as a time of innocence and hoped to find it again.'

'You really are shrewd, aren't you? I'll have to be careful of those sharp little eyes of yours,' he said, staring at her. 'But I suspect you're right, although I hadn't actually worked it out myself until this moment. I'm running from a world I found was destroying me, poisoning my mind. I couldn't bear it any more. I hated the man I had turned into as much as the world I was living in.

'I want to believe in things again—in innocence and goodness and kindness. And people. Most of all, I want to like people and believe in them, without getting laughed at for my gullibility. I wanted to get up in the morning without being afraid that before I went to bed again I'd see people being blown apart or tortured or raped.'

She winced. She couldn't imagine how it must have felt to live that way. 'I hope to God I never have to face a world like that,' she said slowly.

His face sombre, he said, 'I hope to God you don't too.' Then he gave a violent start and jumped to his feet as the reel on his fishing-rod began to spin and there was a sound of splashing in the river. 'I've got something on my line!'

Kit leapt up too, watching with held breath as he fought whatever was on the end of the line, then triumphantly reeled in a large trout, silver-scaled and glittering with rainbow colours in the misty light.

Joe solemnly weighed in on portable scales while some of the other fishermen along the river watched, then he slid the trout into his net, which was suspended in the river so that anything he caught which he did not intend to eat could be kept alive in the water and thrown back later.

'Time for lunch,' he said then, looking at his watch before washing his hands to get rid of the smell of the fish. 'Hungry?'

'I do seem to be, yes,' she admitted, surprised by the fact.

'It's the fresh air. I could eat a horse myself.'

'I hope that isn't what you've brought! I'd rather starve than eat a horse!'

He grinned at her. 'Quite right too. Why do we say these things? Laziness and habit. Don't worry, I haven't brought a horse—something much nicer. I think you'll enjoy it. Look, you sit there; I won't be long.'

He vanished towards his car which he had parked in a small car park above the river. When he came back he was carrying a large wicker picnic basket and a small folding table, which he set up on the flat path beside the river. He draped this with a Stuart tartan rug, on which he laid out knives and forks, plates and glasses before he unpacked the picnic basket, producing a bewildering array of food—rough French terrine of rabbit and prunes, cold legs of chicken, a game pie, cheese, a box of crisp salad, a bottle of French dressing, a baguette, some apples, and a tub of strawberries which must have cost the earth at that time of year.

Kit's mouth was open. 'This is not a picnic—it's a feast!'

He pulled the pièce de résistance out—a bottle of champagne—and popped the cork, hurriedly pouring the fizzing wine into their glasses.

Lifting his glass, he murmured, 'To a peaceful and happy life for both of us.'

'For all of us,' Kit corrected, toasting him and smiling.

He nodded. 'Amen to that.' He sipped his champagne, eyes half-shut. 'Mmm...good.' He put down his glass and picked up a knife, gesturing to the terrine. 'Can I cut you a slice?'

'A small one,' she said. 'It looks wonderful; I love those rough French terrines, especially made with rabbit.'

The meal was eaten with leisurely enjoyment, then they drank some coffee from a flask that Joe had brought before they both packed everything away, the remains of the food back into the picnic basket, the debris into the bag Joe had provided for it.

They had drunk all the champagne; the empty bottle was tucked back into the picnic basket along with the empty coffee-flask. Then Joe took the basket and table back to the car while Kit leaned back in her canvas chair, half-asleep.

The afternoon was half-over by then. She was pleasantly relaxed; she had had a wonderful day, far more enjoyable than she had expected, and she was sorry when Joe said they should be leaving soon, but there was no doubt that the day was ending.

The spring light was darkening on the water, birds flew and called among the trees, and all the other fishermen and their families were packing up and going. Soon dusk would fall and the river bank would be quiet, except for the scurrying of the little animals that lived there, the swoop and blood-curdling cries of the owls preying on them.

'Glad you came?' Joe asked, smiling at her.

'Very glad. I feel as if I've been somewhere far away.' It was a strange experience; body and mind were refreshed and invigorated, yet she was sleepy and felt heavy.

By the time they got back to their block of flats night had descended, and unbelievably Kit felt hungry again.

'Would you like some supper?' she asked Joe.

'Love some. I hoped you'd ask—I was just about to drop a hint!' he said, following her into the lift and up to her flat.

She laughed, making a face at him. 'And I bet you'd have done it, too!'

'You can believe it. Fair's fair. I provided the lunch, after all. I believe in sharing everything fifty-fifty.'

'So do I,' she said, her face sobering as she thought of Liam. If only *he* did! But he was a very different man. She thought back over their years together—he had never let her into his secret thoughts, never confided in her, let her find out what went on inside his head.

'You look sad—what are you thinking about?' Joe asked gently, and she shook the bitter memories away.

'I was wondering what to cook!'

She knew that he didn't believe her; his eyes were wry but he didn't press the point.

'Can I help?' he asked, following her into the kitchen.

'You can make some coffee while I cook some eggs.' They had scrambled eggs with a few scraps of smoked salmon she had left in the fridge, served with snippets of toast, and followed that with some cheese and biscuits left over from the picnic.

They drank their coffee in the sitting room, talking, listening to an old recording of Elgar, the music very English, nostalgic and poignant.

Kit asked Joe about his book and he talked easily, amusing and sad by turns, then suddenly broke off with a yawn.

'Sorry, I must be more tired than I'd thought.' He looked at the clock. 'Good heavens, look at the time! No wonder I'm tired—it's gone eleven. I'd better go. Thanks for a lovely day, Kit.'

'Thank you. I had a marvellous time.' She walked to the front door with him and he paused to look down at her, smiling.

'Do I get a goodnight kiss?'

She hesitated, then stood on tiptoe and kissed his cheek, the way he had kissed hers after the antiques fair. But before she could move away again Joe bent quickly and caught her mouth, his lips warm and firm. The kiss was over before she needed to decide how to respond and he straightened.

'Goodnight, Kit.'

He walked away towards the lift; she watched him go, her hand instinctively lifted to her mouth, one finger tracing her lower lip.

She didn't know how she felt. She liked him, but her world hadn't tilted when he'd kissed her; her heart hadn't turned over and over, the way it had the first time Liam had kissed her.

Joe went into the lift, the doors closed after him and Kit began to close the door—only to stop, her nerves jumping, as someone moved in the shadows of the stairs leading up to the next floor.

'Who's that?' she called shakily, and the shape came down into the light of the landing.

It was Liam. Kit drew a sharp breath, stiffening as she took in his black sweater and jeans, which had made him almost invisible in the unlit corner of the stairs.

'What were you doing lurking about up there?' she demanded in an accusing voice.

'I wasn't lurking,' he bit out, his face a taut mask. 'I was being discreet. I was just coming to the front door when I heard voices inside the flat and realised you were saying goodbye to someone, so I thought you'd rather I waited until your visitor had gone before I showed up.'

She looked at her watch. 'It's quarter past eleven! A bit late for a social call!'

'I'm sorry, I need to talk to you urgently. Can I come in?'

He moved forward, and she stepped back because he was too close for comfort and she had the feeling that if she argued, tried to refuse him admittance, he might push past her anyway and she was in no mood for direct confrontation at this hour.

'What do you want to talk about?'

He didn't answer her; he simply walked past, and Kit shut the front door, her nerves prickling.

'Honestly, Liam! What is all this?'

Liam walked into the sitting room and stood on the hearth rug, staring around as if looking for clues to whatever she and Joe had been doing that evening. His bleak eyes took in the coffee-cups, the open box of after-dinner mints, the rumpled cushions on the sofa.

'Had a good time today?' he asked, his lips crooked with cynicism.

'Yes, thank you,' she said warily. How dared he look at her like that? He had no right to sit in judgement on her.

'You haven't been answering your phone all day. Where have you been since nine o'clock this morning?'

Her green eyes opened wider. Had he been ringing her all day? 'Joe took me fishing.'

'Fishing?' He didn't sound as if he believed her. Her chin went up and she looked at him defiantly.

'That's right. We've been on the river bank all day, fishing. We had a picnic and Joe caught several trout—I've got two in my fridge if you want to see them. I might cook them for dinner tomorrow night.'

'For you and Ingram?'

The curt question made her even more tense. 'Maybe,' she bit back, although in fact she had already decided to give both trout to Paddy to cook for herself and Fred.

Liam's cold eyes flicked over her, from her tousled silvery hair, freed now from the velvet band that had held it back all day and curling loosely around her face, down over her sweater and jeans, to her feet in white socks.

'You look like a teenager!' he accused.

'Thanks for the compliment!'

'It isn't meant to be one. You aren't a teenager, you're a grandmother, for God's sake. Act like one.'

Angry heat ran up her face; she glared at him, shaking with fury. 'Don't you try to define me by labels. I'm not a teenager or a grandmother, actually—I'm myself; I'm Kit Randall, a person of sound mind—and so far, thank heaven—body, and I'll do whatever I like. I don't have to ask anybody's permission or approval, so will you stop trying to order me around and make me feel guilty for enjoying myself?'

His eyes flashed. 'One day I'll—' He broke off.

'One day you'll what? Hit me?' She had read it in his eyes, the desire to do violence, and her nerves prickled. 'That's what you were going to say, wasn't it? I might have known you'd sink to that level sooner or later. If you can't get your own way with a woman, hit her—that's typical male thinking, isn't it?'

'I'm not a typical male,' he bit out. 'Although it did cross my mind just now when you were ranting on at me that a good smack wouldn't do you any harm. But I don't hit women, whatever the provocation, so you're quite safe from me, don't worry.'

'I'm not worrying. I'm just bloody mad, and I warn you, if you ever did lay a finger on me I'd hit you right back.'

His mouth twisted. 'I know you would.'

They stared at each other, breathing audibly, as if they had been fighting physically instead of verbally.

Kit drew a painful breath. 'You still haven't told me why you're here, what's so important that it can't wait until the morning.'

His voice sounded abstracted, remote. 'I won't be at work for a couple of days; I'm going away.'

There was nothing unusual about that—he often went on buying trips to auctions in other parts of the country. 'Oh? Where?'

'Wales. I've just heard about someone with a house full of antiques who wants to raise some money quickly, so I'm getting in there before anyone else hears about it.'

'Who told you about it?'

He turned a cool, shuttered face to her. 'Cary.'

She stiffened, her eyes narrowing, bright green and jealous.

He casually said, 'Several times when Cary was working in the V&A she helped this woman's husband identify clocks that he had bought in France and Italy. When the husband died his wife found herself short of cash but with a house full of antiques—she wants to sell most of them, but there is so much there, and she needs expert advice on what's what and how much it is worth. She didn't know where to start or who to trust.

'Her husband was obsessed with clocks and had hundreds of them. As she knew Cary quite well, and felt she could trust her, she rang her to ask for help, but of course Cary is only an expert where clocks are concerned; she might not recognise the true value of some of the other stuff, so Cary asked me to come along.'

Flatly Kit said, 'So you are going to Wales with Cary?' She felt as if someone had stuck a knife in her and was twisting it round and round. She had to fight to stop the pain showing on her face or in her voice.

He nodded. 'First thing tomorrow. We have to move fast before this woman invites someone else to view the stuff before we get there. She's in a hurry; she won't wait long.'

Carefully Kit asked, 'But surely the estate has been valued for probate?' She wanted to sound calm and businesslike; instead her voice came out stilted, unreal. She only hoped Liam didn't notice.

He nodded impatiently. 'Of course it was—but they largely worked on the husband's estimates of what his possessions were worth. He had a pretty heavy insurance on the house and contents, with a list of what was there; the lawyers used that as their guideline in estimating what the estate was worth. But that list is only a rough guide. Values shift all the time, you know that. Some pieces will go for less, others for more than the estimated value.

'The widow doesn't know much about antiques—they were her husband's hobby, not her own. In fact Cary says the woman resented the amount of money he spent on antiques; they quarrelled about it all the time, and Cary suspects she'll enjoy selling his collection, just to get her own back.' He grimaced. 'You talked about typical male thinking just now—well, this is typical female thinking! Vindictive even beyond the grave.'

'Oh, thanks!' Kit muttered, eyeing him with rage. 'It sounds to me as if this woman had a lot of justification for being angry—her husband apparently spent so much on his hobby that when he died she was left without money, just a house full of antiques! How would you feel in her place?'

'I'm not arguing with you—you're biased.' Liam shrugged. 'I must go; I'll have to be up early tomorrow.'

'Are you driving into Wales?'

'Yes, of course. I'll take my estate car—then I can bring back anything portable that I buy.'

'So you aren't going with Cary, then?'

His grey eyes met hers. 'Yes, she's coming with me in my car,' he said coolly, and turned to walk back to the door. 'I've dropped a note into the office; all my appointments have to be cancelled for the next three days. I should be back by Wednesday. If this is going to take any longer I'll ring and let you know. We'll be staying at a local pub called the Green Dragon in a village whose name I can't pronounce.'

He pulled a piece of paper out of his pocket and handed it to her. 'That's the address and telephone number. If I'm urgently needed you can contact me there.'

Kit held the piece of paper without looking at it. She couldn't think of anything to say. Was he going to be sharing a room with Cary Burnaby, or weren't they sleeping together yet? Well, if they weren't, no doubt Liam would soon change that. At this pub in the village whose name he couldn't pronounce he and Cary would be sleeping under one roof; how long would it take him to get her into bed? Kit wouldn't care to put a bet on it.

She stood in the hallway, struggling with pain and misery, and watched Liam walk away.

I could kill him! she thought, closing the door to shut out the sight of him. I could kill him!

CHAPTER FIVE

IN FACT Liam was away for the whole week, and Kit's imagination was working overtime on what he and Cary Burnaby were doing all that time.

And she wasn't the only one, as she discovered the following Thursday when she overheard Fred and Paddy chatting while they were working in the sale room on items which would be included in the next auction to be held there.

'With Cary Burnaby?' Fred sounded shocked. 'He has gone away with Cary Burnaby? Are you sure? Who told you? Not Kit...'

Freezing in the doorway, Kit hardly dared to breathe in case they noticed her presence.

Paddy paused to stick a number on a Victorian chaise longue upholstered in red velvet. 'Of course it wasn't Kit! I don't suppose she knows! No. I found out by accident. I noticed her shop was closed yesterday as I walked past it, so I asked the lady who runs a wool shop next door if Cary was ill and she said no, Cary had gone to Wales for a few days on business.'

Fred clicked his tongue disapprovingly. 'I'd never have believed it! Poor Kit.'

Kit slipped out of the room and went back to her own office to stand at the window, staring out at the traffic moving sluggishly past in the street below. The words burned in her mind. 'Poor Kit', Fred had said pityingly, and she felt sick with pain and humiliation.

What was it that people always said about eaves-droppers? That they heard no good of themselves? Well, she hadn't, anyway. Everyone who worked in the auction rooms must know about her and Liam. Oh, people might not know for sure exactly what had happened between them—but it was well known that they had been seeing a lot of each other out of office hours, and probably people suspected that they had not just been holding hands in the moonlight.

Or maybe, at their ages, nobody suspected them of going to bed together?

She turned to look into a little Venetian mirror which she kept hanging on the wall above her desk, reflecting the window behind her, giving her glimpses of the changing sky; the lilac tree which grew outside, and which was budding now, would soon be bursting into green leaf.

Her own reflection filled the mirror as she leaned towards it; she looked with bitter resignation at her silver-grey hair, the lines that time was beginning to etch on her skin, the soft crêpe of the skin on her throat.

It's barely noticeable except to me! she thought quickly. You have to look closely to see the lines, the ageing of my neck, especially when I take the time to do my make-up carefully. I can cover up those lines, smooth over the faint wrinkling of my throat.

Who do you think you're kidding? she mocked herself. Face it—you're getting old.

Fifty-two isn't old, it's middle-aged! she argued at once, but her inner voice retorted, Well, whatever it is, why on earth would any man want to go to bed with you now?

Liam did! she reminded herself, her eyes half closing at the memory of their passionate nights together.

He didn't want to marry you, though, her mind coldly pointed out. Or even live with you. He didn't want to be tied to you in any way. He never made a commitment to you. And now he has met a younger woman and he's dumped you. Face it. It's all over for you. You're too old to fall in love, too old to feel desire or need. Too old.

The phone rang and she jumped out of her skin, gasping, then picked up the phone and breathlessly said, 'Hello?'

'Kit?'

She was so off balance that she couldn't place the voice for a moment. 'Yes, who is this?'

'It's Joe.' And he sounded taken aback, even hurt, because she hadn't recognised his voice at once.

She pulled herself together. 'Oh, hi! How are you?'

'Fine—how are *you*?'

'I'm OK.'

'You don't sound it. You sound husky, as if you've been crying, or are getting a cold. I hope you're not; I was going to ask you out tonight.'

He was very quick, very shrewd. She tried to sound light-hearted, casual. 'I don't think I'm getting a cold. I was working, that's all; my mind was miles away.'

'Fine—then will you?'

He had lost her again. 'Will I what?'

He laughed. 'Wake up, Kit! Will you come out with me tonight? I thought we could go and see the new Tom Cruise film—it's had very good reviews.'

'I'd love to,' she said, without needing to think—anything to get out of her flat, be occupied, not have time to dwell on what Liam might or might not be doing in Wales. And, anyway, it did her battered ego no end of good to know that someone ten years younger than she was wanted to spend time with her.

Joe's voice warmed; he sounded very pleased. 'Great—I'll pick you up at your flat at six-thirty—we'll go and eat first, shall we? The film starts at eight-thirty—we should have time to eat. Where would you like to go—Indian, Chinese, Mexican?'

'What's wrong with English food?' she teased.

'The English restaurants don't open until seven-thirty. We'd never have time to eat in one.'

'So they don't. OK, then, let's eat Chinese.'

'Perfect, I love it.' Joe was as open-minded and cosmopolitan about food as he was about everything else. He was the perfect companion when you were feeling low—he was so interested in the world, in ideas, in what was happening now. She enjoyed his company and she liked him more the better she got to know him.

But her conscience reproached her later when she was getting ready, putting on a pleated heather tweed skirt, a vivid green sweater with a roll neck, brushing her hair until it shone like spun silver, putting on make-up and perfume.

Was it fair to Joe to go on seeing him when she was in love with another man?

She wouldn't want to hurt him. She had been too badly hurt herself to want to do that to anyone else, especially someone she liked as much as Joe.

Oh, come on, he isn't serious! she told herself scornfully. Joe is ten years younger than you. If you're too old for Liam, you're certainly much too old for Joe.

Joe is using you just as much as you're using him. Joe's a newcomer in town; he's lonely, he wants company—he's been frank about that. He isn't going to get too involved; you won't hurt him.

But maybe I should talk to him? Her mouth twisted ironically. Oh, yeah? Say what? Look, Joe, don't fall in love with me because I will never care that way about you?

Can you see yourself saying that? Can you imagine his expression? He would either be embarrassed or, even worse, would have a problem trying not to laugh.

And, anyway, he knows about Liam already; he knows you love someone else; he's no fool.

She looked at her reflection with bleak disfavour. The only fool around here is you, Kit Randall! she thought crossly.

When Joe arrived he was in a hurry to get to the Chinese restaurant but he still managed to notice how she looked and tell her that he loved the green sweater.

'It exactly matches the colour of your eyes. Has anyone ever told you that your eyes are exactly like a cat's?'

'Not if they wanted to stay friends of mine!'

'Oh, but I love cats!' he protested, laughing, as he unlocked his car.

Her face turned serious. 'Don't love me, Joe,' she said, half to herself, but aloud so that he could hear her.

He turned to look at her, his own face sobering. For a second they stared at each other in silence, then he said, 'Mustn't I, Kit?'

She shook her head, her mouth quivering. He looked at it, touched the pink line of it with one finger, very briefly, very lightly. 'Well, I'll try not to love you, Kit. Thank you for warning me.'

He held the door open for her, and she got into the passenger seat and closed her eyes, a burning pain behind her lids. He hadn't laughed or looked embarrassed. Surely he wasn't beginning to get serious about her? A quiver of uncertainty ran through her.

She liked Joe. Couldn't she try to do more than like him? She remembered the way he had just looked at her, and felt sadness. Liam didn't love her; there was no future for her with him. Might there be one with Joe? She wished she hadn't said anything, wished she could call the words back.

Joe slid into the driving seat and Kit whispered, 'I'm sorry, Joe.'

He turned to look at her, his face masked by shadow. Quietly he said, 'Kit, the first night we met—do you remember? You told me that you weren't free; you were very honest. I can't say I didn't know the score, Kit, but I was lonely here, and it didn't seem to matter in the beginning.'

She looked quickly at him, her green eyes wide and anxious. 'It doesn't matter now, does it, Joe?'

His gaze was frank and direct. 'I only know I'd miss you like hell if I didn't see you again. You've become an important part of my life very quickly.'

She bit her lip. 'Joe...'

He started the engine. 'Oh, don't you worry about me, Kit. I'm a big boy now; I won't come crying all over you. But if you could go on seeing me now and then...just as friends, nothing more, Kit—I don't know what I'd do with myself if I lost you as a friend.'

She blindly put a hand over one of his where it rested on the wheel. 'Of course we're friends! And I'd miss you too. I just wanted to...'

He picked up her hand and kissed it softly. 'Put me straight? OK, Kit, I know exactly where I stand so you needn't feel guilty or fret.'

After that fraught beginning they had a very enjoyable evening; the meal was good, the film even better, and their talk ranged over a dozen different subjects, easily and without a shadow of any kind on Joe's face or in his voice.

*   *   *

Next day Kit got a phone call from Geraldine van Dijk, Liam's married daughter.

'I've been trying to get hold of my father all week—is he away, do you know?'

Kit explained that he was in Wales on a buying trip, and gave her the name and telephone number Liam had left with her, then said, 'How are you, Geraldine, and your husband and little girl?'

'We're all fine, thanks. How are you?'

'Oh, I'm fine too. It seems a long time since we last met.'

'I hope I'll be seeing you again soon. My husband has to come to London in a week's time to attend a dentistry conference. He wasn't booked to go but a colleague who was going has just had an accident and won't be fit enough in time, so Hans was asked to take his place. I thought we might come with him, and stay with Dad for a couple of days while Hans is at the conference.'

'Liam will be delighted to have you home for a while.'

'But how long is he going to be in Wales?'

'Oh, he's due back any day now. He'll certainly be back by the time you get here. I hope I'll see something of you while you're here—you must come out to lunch with me, you and little Vanessa.'

'I'd love that,' said Geraldine warmly.

Kit was smiling as she put the phone down; she liked Liam's daughter, although she had wondered from time to time if Geraldine resented her. Family relationships were always hard to understand from outside, but Kit knew that Geraldine adored her father and that he was very attached to her. And to Vanessa, of course. Liam wasn't exactly a doting grandfather, but he was gravely attentive to Vanessa whenever she was with him; he was the sort of man who treated children as if they were adults and yet was gently indulgent with them.

Maybe the news of Geraldine's arrival would make Liam hurry back from Wales? Kit sighed, picking up the sale catalogue she was putting together. She missed him badly. It seemed a long time since she'd last seen him.

That evening as she was tossing a salad to go with her supper of grilled salmon steak her doorbell jangled and she jumped.

Joe! she thought, smiling, and went to open the door. She had told him she would be busy that evening, but she had half expected that he would ignore the warning.

'I might have known you'd...' Her voice died as she met Liam's grey gaze. 'Oh, hello,' she said huskily. 'I thought you were somebody else.'

'Expecting company?' His eyes narrowed, hard and cold as pebbles on a wintry beach. 'Ingram, I suppose?'

Her flush deepened. He was leaning on her door-frame, freshly shaved and with his hair smoothly brushed, wearing a dark suit and striped blue and white shirt, his silk tie the colour of deep blue hyacinths, a colour which gave a new depth and colour to his smoky grey eyes. Her pulses began to drum at the sight of him.

'When did you get back?' she asked him. 'Geraldine rang me. I gave her your number in Wales; did she manage to catch you?'

He was staring at her intently—she hoped he couldn't read her expression, wasn't picking up the fast beating of her heart, the disturbed drag of her breathing. She felt as if she hadn't seen him for a lifetime. What was he thinking? That face of his was a mask again, inscrutable, unreadable.

'Yes, just as I was about to leave the Green Dragon to drive back here I got a call from her,' he said quietly. 'She told you she and Vanessa are coming to stay next week?' He looked over her shoulder into her flat, his brows lifting sardonically. 'I wanted to hear how the week had gone at work; do we have to talk on your doorstep? And is that something burning?'

She looked blankly at him. 'What?' Then her nose wrinkled. 'Oh, no! My salmon!' She ran back into her kitchen and groaned as she saw smoke coming out of the grill. Grabbing her oven gloves, she pulled the grill-pan out. The pink fish was burnt black. 'It's ruined,' she wailed.

Liam contemplated it. 'It's my fault for distracting you while you were cooking it. Chuck it away and let me buy you dinner, or are you expecting Ingram later? I can see you were only cooking one piece of salmon—does that mean he isn't coming to dinner?'

She was very tempted, but an evening alone with him would be an ordeal, so she shook her head, turning off the grill before the whole stove caught fire.

'No, he isn't, but if you've driven all the way from Wales you must be tired. It wasn't your fault I burnt the salmon; I just forgot about it. I've got some cheese and eggs; I can make myself an omelette.' She dumped the salmon into her waste bin under the kitchen sink, saying over her shoulder, 'So how did the Welsh trip go? Did you get anything special? Did Cary Burnaby come back with you?'

Liam gave her a smouldering stare, then walked out of the room without answering. Kit was rooted to the spot, shaking with a strange mixture of pain and rage.

How dared he walk out on her like that?

She waited to hear the front door open and close, but it didn't; instead she heard Liam walking about in her flat—what on earth was he doing? Then he came back through the kitchen door and held out her dark brown winter coat.

'Get this on and stop arguing.'

Taken aback, she mumbled, 'I've made salad.'

'Put it in the fridge—it won't spoil.'

She gazed helplessly around the room, her mind in utter confusion. 'The kitchen is a mess; I should tidy up.'

'Leave it until the morning.'

She looked at him, her green eyes glittering. 'Stop giving me orders!'

'Stop wasting my time!' He gestured with the coat. 'Come on, Kit; put this on and we'll go.'

She looked at him ruefully. She was going to give in and she knew it. But she still dragged her feet, angry with herself for being so weak-willed where he was concerned. 'I need to get ready—put on some make-up, do my hair.'

'You look fine just as you are.'

She met his insistent stare and gave in, but first she covered her salad bowl with cling film and put it into the fridge. It gave her some sense of being in control.

He took her to one of their favourite restaurants, a French one right in the centre of town—the place he had taken Cary Burnaby to one evening, she thought. The last time Kit had been there herself she had been with Joe, a few nights ago.

The head waiter came up smiling and bowing. 'Mrs Randall, you left your gloves here on Tuesday night.' He had them in his hand—black leather gloves she had worn only a couple of times so far. 'I meant to ring you if you didn't come in again soon.'

'I wondered what I'd done with them!' she said, laughing. 'I've been hunting high and low—thank you, Ivo.' Then she saw Liam's eyes and her heart jumped into her throat.

The head waiter didn't notice anything. Chatting cheerfully, he showed them to a table in a corner and gave them each a menu. 'Can I get you a drink while you choose?'

'A dry Martini, please,' Kit said huskily.

'Scotch,' Liam bit out.

'With water or ginger?'

'Straight.'

The head waiter vanished and she looked blindly down at her menu.

'You were here with Ingram, I suppose?' Liam muttered.

'Yes.' She was bewildered again, lost and confused. Liam was full of rage—she could see that clearly enough, hear it in his voice. But why was he so furious? He had brought Cary Burnaby here—why shouldn't she have come here with Joe?

'Do you see him every night now?'

She looked up, suddenly angry too. 'Why shouldn't I? You just spent a week in Wales with Cary Burnaby. Why shouldn't I see another man?'

He stared back at her, his features taut, his skin pale. 'I don't like him.'

If she hadn't been so hurt and angry she would have laughed. 'Well, I do!'

Liam swallowed; she saw his throat move as if he had something stuck in it which he couldn't dislodge.

'You aren't sleeping with him, are you, Kit?'

'Are you sleeping with her?'

Across the table their eyes met, like the eyes of deadly enemies with drawn swords between them.

'No,' Liam said with force.

She felt relief seep through her, but she didn't betray it. Coolly she said, 'Really? I thought that was the whole point of going away with her.'

'The whole point of going to Wales was to value a house full of antiques,' Liam said angrily, and then the head waiter came back with their drinks and asked if they had chosen their meal yet.

'Melon and sole,' Kit said without looking at the menu. It was what she usually had and she was in no mood to experiment tonight.

'The sole off the bone, of course,' the head waiter said, knowing her tastes.

'Yes, please.' She didn't have the patience to spend ages dissecting a fish.

Liam ordered just as automatically. 'Consommé and the turbot.'

'And the vegetables?'

'Just asparagus for me,' Liam said. 'And some boiled new potatoes. What about you?' he asked Kit without looking at her.

'A green salad, please; no potatoes.'

'A green salad,' repeated the head waiter, writing fast.

She nodded, managed a smile. 'Thank you.'

Liam added, 'And a bottle of Chablis.'

When the man had gone Liam picked up his glass of whisky, drank it in one swallow, and looked around for a waiter. 'I need another drink,' he muttered.

He rarely drank much; she watched him uncertainly. 'What *is* wrong with you?'

His eyes came back to her with a flash which had something of desperation in it. 'I can't...' The words trailed off; he moved his wide shoulders in a shrug of angry confusion. 'God...I don't know.' He looked around. 'Where the hell is that wine waiter? If I can't have another whisky I could at least have some wine.'

She involuntarily put a hand across the table to touch one of his and felt his fingers quiver violently as if he had just got an electric shock. She quickly withdrew her hand, shaken by his reaction.

'You aren't going to get drunk, are you, Liam?' She tried a little teasing persuasion. 'Please don't; I'd hate it, and you'd have a very bad headache tomorrow. You know you always pay for it if you drink more than a couple of glasses of wine!'

His grey eyes rested on her broodingly. 'Just like a woman. First you drive me to drink, then you reproach me for it.'

'Just like a man—blame women for everything you do!' she threw back at him, smiling.

The waiter arrived with their first course and Liam said to him, 'We ordered some wine; could you see that we get it at once?'

'Of course, sir.'

Kit's melon was delicious; she concentrated on it for a few moments, and Liam did the same with his beef consommé, a deep golden liquid dressed with some matchstick-sized fragments of vegetables—carrot, courgette, green pepper. The wine arrived, was tasted and pronounced acceptable; the waiter poured them both a glass.

Finishing his soup, Liam played with the bread roll on his plate, his head bent.

'So what did you buy in Wales?' Kit asked, and he began to tell her what the house had contained, what he had acquired.

'I've talked to Fred and the men; they'll be driving to Wales to pick it all up on Monday, and I'll be going back with them to check the stuff into the van.'

'Is Cary still there? In Wales?'

'No, she's gone to London, to somebody's wedding.'

Had they quarrelled? Hadn't the week been a success? Kit watched him hungrily, wishing she could read his mind, wishing he would talk to her frankly, not keep so much to himself. She sipped some of her Chablis, which had a pale golden colour and a crisp taste. Maybe she would get more out of Liam when he had drunk another couple of glasses?

The waiter removed their plates and the second course arrived. 'So, tell me what's happened here,' Liam prompted.

She told him what had come into the auction rooms that week, outlined the contents of the catalogue for the next sale, and he listened intently. He seemed to have calmed down. He didn't drink much of the wine after all; they didn't finish the bottle. Instead they sat for ages over several cups of black coffee, and by the time they left Liam was perfectly sober, but she still insisted that he shouldn't drive home. They shared a taxi, which dropped her off first and went on to take him home.

On Monday he and Fred and the removal team drove to Wales and returned late that night with a van full of furniture, clocks, some porcelain and glass and, to Kit's delight, a marvellous collection of German and French dolls, one of them eighteenth century and very valuable.

Toys were one of Kit's specialities; she would have a wonderful time cataloguing this collection. She only wished that she could buy some of it for herself, but most of it was too valuable for her. She might manage to acquire one doll, though.

Geraldine and her little girl arrived on Tuesday morning and came in to the auction rooms on Wednesday to see the toys.

'Don't touch, darling!' Geraldine warned Vanessa, who was wide-eyed with delight as she looked at the dolls.

Kit had hidden a modern one among them—a present for Vanessa. She picked it up and handed it to her now.

'This one is nice; she talks.'

She showed the little girl how to press the doll's back; it obediently said, 'Ma-ma,' and Vanessa laughed excitedly.

'How about lunch?' asked Geraldine. 'Dad's too busy today, he said, but I hoped you might be able to come.'

'It will have to be quick,' Kit told her apologetically. 'I must be back by two—I've an appointment with someone who's bringing some silver to be valued.'

They had lunch in an open-air café in the park, five minutes' walk away. The set meal of the day was spaghetti carbonara; Vanessa loved it but had to be enveloped in a huge white bib before she was allowed to eat. Afterwards, while the two women drank coffee, the little girl skipped round the lawns outside the café, singing tunelessly to herself, her doll clutched to her.

Spring was advancing fast, trees in leaf giving a green haze to the view, daffodils blaring gold trumpets in their regimental ranks under the trees. You were suddenly aware of the birds constantly flying to and fro with bits of nest-making material in their beaks, or singing defiantly on branches or rooftops, and when you breathed it in the air had a crisp sweetness, more potent than any man-made perfume.

Kit looked up at the blue sky with pleasure. The older she got, the more she welcomed spring and the harder winters became for her. She was conscious of an ache in her back from sitting on a hard plastic chair for too long.

'What's going on with you and Dad?' Geraldine asked, and Kit looked sharply at her, startled.

'What do you mean?'

Geraldine's face was wry. 'Oh, come on, Kit, you know what I mean. Dad's like a dog with a thorn in his paw—as touchy as hell—and you're obviously under some sort of strain. Have you two quarrelled?'

Kit flushed; she could hardly tell Liam's daughter the truth—how did you say to someone, Your father refuses to marry me; he just wants to sleep with me?

'Not exactly...' she said slowly. 'It's more... a disagreement.'

'About something important?' Geraldine was frowning, trying to understand.

Kit sighed. 'I'm afraid so. He's not an easy man, your father.'

'No, he isn't,' the younger woman agreed, then gave her a pleading look. 'Kit, don't give up on him. I think you've been great for him—we all do—I mean me and Hans, and my brother, Felix, and his wife; we all think Dad's been much happier since you two got together.

'He had a tough time, you know, with Mum all those years, and he was marvellous; he put up with so much, and he was always there for us. If it hadn't been for Dad we would have had a miserable childhood; he deserves some happiness at last. I know he can be difficult, but he needs you. Give him another chance.'

Kit kept very still, hiding her eagerness. She was dying to ask her a hundred questions, but if she was too openly curious it might have the opposite effect—she might shut Geraldine up altogether.

Carefully she said, 'I remember when you were little he was always the one who took you to school and collected you again. And it was always him who turned up at prize-givings and sports days. Your mother was . . . not very strong . . . was she?'

Geraldine laughed shortly. 'That's a very polite way of putting it. She was a hopeless alcoholic, you mean.'

CHAPTER SIX

KIT felt as if someone had punched her in the stomach. She stared at Geraldine, her eyes stretching until they hurt.

Geraldine was looking away, across the room, at her little girl. Her mouth was quivering as if she was going to cry.

Huskily, she said, 'I'm surprised you don't know, Kit. I thought Dad would have told you all about it. Anyway, I'm glad you know now. Felix and I . . . well, we both hate having a secret like that. We still never talk about it, you know. Dad drilled it into us never to tell anyone. It was like having someone in the family who had an unmentionable disease. It made our lives a misery when we were kids. We couldn't even bring friends home because you never knew how she would be, even at ten in the morning.'

Kit's mouth opened in a gasp. 'Ten in the morning?'

Geraldine glanced at her, grimacing. 'Oh, you don't know what it's like living with a drunk. The nearest thing to it is living on the slopes of a volcano. You never know when it's going to erupt, or how bad the eruption will be.

'First thing in the morning, if she was up at all— and she often wasn't, but if she was—she was always bad-tempered. We prayed she wouldn't get up because we knew she would turn on us for the slightest thing. We had to whisper or she would yell that we were making too much noise; we had to tiptoe about; we couldn't play anywhere in the house.

'Once she had had a few drinks she would change; she'd be in a very good mood for a while, almost normal, but she never stopped at a few drinks, so it wouldn't be long before she changed again. We got to know all the phases. You could tell at a glance what phase she was in ... I don't know which was worst—when she was drowned drunk and just lay about in utter torpor, or when she was noisy and aggressive, shouting and yelling, throwing things, breaking things, hitting people...'

'You? She didn't hit you and Felix?' Kit was shaken to her roots—she couldn't imagine the delicate, pale, gentle-seeming Claudia actually striking someone, especially her own child.

'All the time,' Geraldine said, her eyes clearly stinging with tears. 'Dad protected us when he was in the house, and he tried to make sure we were never left alone with her. We weren't wealthy people but we always had a nanny; it never occurred to me when I was little but, of course, our nanny was also there to keep an eye on my mother. But it wasn't always possible to keep us away from her, and her mood changed so fast that you never knew what she would do next; she was cunning, very deceptive.'

'It's all so incredible,' Kit whispered. Surely Geraldine must be exaggerating? Kit hadn't seen much of Claudia, but what Geraldine was saying was in direct contradiction of everything she remembered about her.

Geraldine sighed. 'Yes, I know. I don't suppose you guessed any of this—most people never suspected what was going on, and Dad went to a lot of trouble to make sure nobody saw her when she was on a drinking jag. He told everyone she was delicate, and it was true enough; in the end, God knows, she ruined her health.'

'Didn't she have treatment? There must have been a reason why she drank. Did she ever have psychoanalysis?'

'Dad tried everything—phychiatrists, drying-out clinics, therapy groups; he tried to get her to join Alcoholics Anonymous but she wouldn't go to the meetings. She would never admit she had a problem; she kept saying she could stop whenever she really wanted to, but she was lying to herself as much as to us. I remember Dad saying that it was an illness; he told us she couldn't help it; she was sick; we must try to understand...'

Geraldine ran the back of her hand across her eyes then sniffed childishly. 'Sorry. You'd think I would have grown out of crying over it by now, wouldn't you? I suppose I'm in a weepy mood because I'm pregnant again.'

'Are you? Geraldine, that's wonderful,' said Kit warmly, distressed to see her tears. 'Congratulations. I knew you wanted to have another baby.

Is your husband pleased?' It was a relief to talk about something else. Kit was knocked sideways by everything that Geraldine had told her; it threw an entirely new light on the past, on Liam, on his family life.

Why didn't he ever tell me? she thought, but Geraldine had already answered that. Liam was ashamed; the last thing he wanted to do was talk about Claudia, tell anyone.

'Hans is thrilled. We both are.' Geraldine pulled out a handkerchief and dabbed her face, giving a wavering smile. 'We wanted to have another baby while Van's still small; only children can be lonely and they do get spoilt. And it is easier to get your kids over with while you're still young yourself. You're more able to put up with the wear and tear! You need an awful lot of energy to keep up with a two-year-old.'

They both looked at Vanessa who was running round in circles, laughing hysterically.

'Be careful, Van! You'll trip up!' her mother called, leaning forward a little anxiously and poised to get up.

Vanessa slowed, came towards them, and then a few feet away sat down on the path to stare at a caterpillar crawling over the stone.

'Mummy...a paterkiller,' she yelled excitedly. 'Do it bite?'

'No, but don't pick it up, and don't put it in your mouth.'

Kit laughed, and Geraldine gave her a grin. 'Well, she puts everything in her mouth at the moment; I keep having to fish the weirdest stuff out of her. I love kids, but I must say it is nice to talk to a grown-up once in a while. Being alone with Van all day makes me feel that I've suffered brain death. I'd like to get back to work later, while I'm still young enough to restart my career. We only want two children, so I'll still just be in my early thirties by the time they're both at school. Then I can get a job.'

'When's the new baby due?'

'Oh, not for seven months.' Geraldine smoothed a hand down over her flat stomach. 'I don't show yet, do I?'

Kit considered her, then shook her head. 'Not at all, but then you kept your figure for months when you had Vanessa, didn't you?' She stopped talking as she heard the church clock chime. 'Oh, it's two o'clock! I must get back. I'm sorry, Geraldine, but this deal could be very important. Your father will kill me if the client goes off in a huff and sells her silver with someone else.'

'I know what an office tyrant he is!' Geraldine laughed, getting up, and called her little girl, then gave Kit a quick, shy look. 'It was nice to have lunch, Kit. You know, it's the first time I've ever talked about my mother to anyone outside the family. But I don't think of you as being an outsider—you're practically family.'

Kit flushed with pleasure. 'Thanks, Geraldine.'

'You will make up with Dad, won't you?'

Before Kit could answer Vanessa was with them, pulling at her mother's hand. 'I want another go on the swings, Mummy.'

'Another time, darling; we have to go.'

'Oh, Mummy...not yet.'

'We'll come to the park again tomorrow,' Geraldine promised.

They walked back to the auction rooms together in the bright spring sunlight with Vanessa's hands firmly held between the two of them. Every time they came to a kerb they swung her up in the air while they quickly crossed to the other side, and she shrieked with delight and didn't want to be put down.

Liam stood at the window of his office looking down at them. 'Grampa!' Vanessa shouted, and he waved.

Kit felt a painful lurch of feeling deep inside herself; if he had belonged to her this would have been such a marvellous moment for all of them—herself and Liam's daughter with his grand-daughter, coming back in the spring sunshine, and Liam smiling down at them. It would have made them a family.

But Liam did not want to belong to her—he wanted to be free; and now that she knew about his wife's drinking she had some idea why.

What had his marriage done to him?

Throughout the rest of the day she kept coming back to that. What scars had those bitter years left on him? The wounds must have gone deep for him to hide it even now, even from her. She could understand why he would not want the world to know about his wife's drinking, but why couldn't he talk about it to her? She had asked him about his marriage so many times, and he had angrily refused to discuss it.

He must have loved Claudia very much in spite of what she'd put him through, otherwise why would he be so protective of her even after her death?

In bed that night she lay awake, her mind hyperactive, thinking about Claudia—she had seemed such a pale, remote figure during all those years. Kit hadn't really known her, and couldn't fit together all the pieces of this strange jigsaw. There were so many unanswered questions. When had Claudia begun drinking? What had triggered it? What had fed the habit? Surely if she had been happy with Liam she wouldn't have needed to drink? Had their marriage been a disaster from the start? Hadn't Claudia loved him? Had he loved her?

Geraldine had given her one answer to the many questions she had asked Liam over the years. But that answer had opened the door to a new host of questions, and Kit desperately wanted to find the answers to them now.

Geraldine stayed until the end of that week and Kit saw her every day but they never talked about her mother again. Vanessa was with them most of the time, which would have made it difficult, but that was not the only reason why. Geraldine had poured out bitter memories and hurt feelings that afternoon in the park, and had felt a deep relief in doing so, but she had had it drummed into her not to talk about her mother and she wasn't likely to do so again. She had a new life inside her; she preferred to close the door on the past.

Kit had dinner at Liam's house with Geraldine and her husband on the evening before they went back to Holland. Hans amused them all with tales of a dentist's life, but Liam seemed tense and abstracted at times, and often Kit saw his daughter looking anxiously at him and then at her.

When she left that evening Geraldine hugged her and said, 'Don't forget what I said, will you?'

'No,' Kit said, feeling Liam's narrowed eyes on them.

'What are you two plotting?' he asked, and Kit made a face at him.

'Mind your own business.'

Hans laughed. 'Women have their secrets, Liam, you know that!' But Liam did not laugh too. His gaze stayed on Kit's face, searching her for clues.

As she drove home Kit kept remembering that stare, his frown. What had he been thinking? Did he suspect that Geraldine had said something to her about him, or about his dead wife? He would be furious if he knew just how much his daughter had told her.

The next day was Sunday and Kit went fishing with Joe again. It was a tranquil, restful day; she actually fell asleep on the river bank, lying on the tartan rug, a couple of cushions under her head, and woke up to smell trout grilling on a barbecue that Joe had fixed up—a very rough arrangement of stones with skewers balanced across them, the fish laid on top of that.

Kit was ravenous after her sleep and hours of fresh country air; she ate her trout, which was delicious, and then they shared the tossed salad she had brought with her, and followed that with some Cheddar cheese and an apple.

'How's your book coming along?' she asked Joe, who yawned and shrugged.

'I haven't done anything since last week. I'm too busy doing nothing. I've discovered the secret of life—total idleness.'

She laughed, but gave him a concerned glance. 'But don't you have a deadline on the book?'

'The publisher does—I don't.' He poured them both coffee from the flask he had brought along and handed her a bright yellow mug.

She held it between both hands, enjoying the warmth of it on her skin.

Joe took a sip of coffee, closed his eyes and groaned. 'Oh, that is so delicious! This is the life, Kit. I've got plenty of money to live on and I'm happy. Every day I get up and look at the world and feel just great. What more can a guy ask of life? I'll get round to the book sooner or later. There's no urgency.'

'I'd have thought you would be dying to see your pictures beautifully reproduced in a book.'

'Hell, no. Who cares? They're so ephemeral, and life's too short to worry about fame or money. When I think of the way I racketed around the world when I was working ... I hardly ever had as much as a day off, and I saw things that should have knocked me for six, but all I did was reload and shoot another film off. I wasn't taking any of it in, not really; I was looking at mutilation and death without blinking or thinking about what lay behind the pictures I was taking.

'I hate myself when I remember that. It didn't mean anything to me—how could my pictures mean anything either? I was looking at a world in agony, but the agony never showed in my pictures.'

'You're wrong, Joe,' she said fiercely. 'So wrong. Millions of people saw the agony—you showed it to us, Joe. You certainly showed it to me.'

He gave her a twisted little smile. 'Did I? Thanks, Kit, but I'm not sure you're right. Anyway, I've stopped running, and my mind is working.'

He looked soberly at her. 'I have started seeing what I didn't see all those years; I keep remembering; I look at pictures I took and suddenly I feel sick. I feel it was me doing that to those people—and in a way that's true. I wasn't the one doing the killing, but I was a voyeur; I watched it happen and did nothing to stop it.'

She was horrified, worried for him. 'What could you do, Joe? Don't be silly; you were just a witness, you weren't ...'

'An accomplice?' he supplied when she paused. 'Wasn't I, Kit? Wasn't that just what I was? I took those pictures because that was how I earned money—I made money out of other people's pain. I wasn't just a voyeur, I was a pimp too.'

He was so pale, his blue eyes shadowed; Kit was disturbed by how he looked—disturbed and worried about him.

'Joe, that's crazy. You mustn't start thinking like that. Look, if you hadn't been there, do you believe those things wouldn't have happened?'

'I don't know. Maybe, maybe not. If the media weren't around would—?'

She interrupted fiercely, 'There was no photographer around to photograph the massacre of the Innocents by King Herod but it went ahead just the same. And where were you during the Battle of Agincourt? Or how about Waterloo? Why did that happen if you weren't there?'

He held up a hand, laughing. 'OK, OK, you've made your point. But I still have to work things out in my own mind, Kit. In medieval times they called it making your soul—that's what I'm doing. I'm stepping out of life to work out where I am and where I want to go next, and my book can wait.'

It was dark before they left the river bank, and when they got back to the block of flats Kit invited him in for supper, but Joe shook his head.

'Thanks, but I'm tired, Kit; I think I'll have a boiled egg for tea and an early night.' He kissed her on the forehead lightly, as if she were a child. 'Goodnight.'

He had dropped her right outside the main entrance of the block of flats instead of driving into the basement car park first. Kit got out of the car and walked rather stiffly into the building. Lying on the damp grass, even with a rug under her, had been stupid. She was aware of every one of her muscles. Rheumatism, she thought grimly. She got a twinge every now and then on wet days, but to-night it was really painful.

She was tired too, and decided to follow Joe's example and have an early night.

She let herself into her flat and was about to make herself an omelette when the doorbell rang sharply.

Had Joe changed his mind?

She opened the door, her eyes widening as she saw Liam.

'Do you spend every Sunday with him now?' he bit out. 'I saw him drop you off. Very touching, the kiss on the forehead. Is that as far as you've got? He isn't Speedy Gonzales after all, is he?'

'What do you want, Liam?' she said wearily, too tired even to be angry. 'I just had a very enjoyable day—do you have to spoil it?'

His grey eyes glittered. 'While you were enjoying yourself your son and his wife were in an operating theatre.'

'What?' Her colour went in a rush. 'Paul and Claire? What do you mean? What's happened?'

'Car crash,' he muttered, staring at her white face. 'They were in a crash on the motorway... Don't look like that; I'm sorry I snapped. They were both injured, but the operations are over—and the hospital is sounding very optimistic.'

She breathed again but felt her legs buckling under her. She grimly hung on to consciousness;

she must not faint. She had to know about Paul, about the babies.

'How did you hear about it? Who told you? Why you?'

'They tried to get in touch with you first, obviously,' he said, his mouth twisting angrily. 'All day. There was never a reply. In the end, a couple of hours ago, Claire's mother got my number from directory enquiries and rang me. I guessed you were out with Ingram, fishing, but I didn't know where. I worked out that you wouldn't go on fishing after dark, so I came round and parked outside half an hour ago to wait for you.'

Kit's mind was working overtime; she hardly heard what he was saying; she was too busy worrying. 'The children—Ian and Kate. Were they in the car? Are they OK? They weren't . . . injured?'

'No, they were lucky; they came off with a few bruises.'

'Oh, God,' she groaned, feeling sick and icy cold. The room was going round and round.

Liam suddenly grabbed her by the waist with both hands, lifting her right off the floor. Her head whirled. He carried her to the sofa and sat down with her, pushing her head downwards between her legs, his hand a clamp on the back of her neck.

'Breathe deeply,' he ordered roughly.

She breathed, shuddering, and at last he let her up; she fell back against the cushions, her eyes closed.

'I'll get you a drink,' he said curtly.

'No!' She caught his arm, her fingers gripping it tightly. 'Tell me . . . exactly what happened.'

'I don't want you passing out on me again!'

'I won't. Liam, I have to know!'

He stared down at her, hesitating, then said flatly, 'Paul and Claire were driving to spend the day with her mother in York. They ran into fog on the motorway. There was some sort of multiple pile-up; a lorry broke down and a dozen or so cars all crashed into each other. Paul's car ran right into the back of the car in front of him, but luckily the car behind him saw what was happening and braked, otherwise their car would have been sandwiched and they might all have been killed.'

She shuddered, closing her eyes.

'Don't faint!' he muttered, reaching for her.

She leaned on him, feeling his strength supporting her, the warmth of his body stealing into her own cold flesh.

'Go on, Liam, I have to know . . .' she whispered.

'That's all of it. It was only because the car behind them didn't run into them that the children weren't badly hurt; it was just their parents, in the front seats.'

'What sort of injuries?' She was afraid to ask yet she had to know.

'Paul's were typical driver's injuries—broken ribs, a broken arm, fractured shoulderblade, whiplash neck. But he was wearing his seatbelt and it held so his face wasn't seriously damaged when the windscreen went.'

'And Claire?'

She saw Liam's face change, turn grim.

'What?' she cried, shaking.

'She came off the worst—she was wearing a seatbelt too, but it didn't entirely save her. She was showered with broken glass and has bad facial injuries; she has chest injuries too, and her legs were trapped under the crushed front of the car when it came in at her.'

Kit closed her eyes, white-faced and appalled. 'Oh, no! Poor girl.'

'Yes, apparently it took the fire brigade several hours to cut her out of the car. She was in the operating theatre for hours, and her mother is very worried about her.'

'But she will be OK?'

'They hope so, but obviously it is going to be a long process—months—before she's out of hospital.'

'Oh, God, and the children... Where are they now? Who's looking after them?'

'Claire's mother. She was the first to hear the news—amazingly enough, she saw film of the crash on the local TV news and recognised the car. It must have been a terrific shock; Molly said the bonnet had crumpled up like old tin foil; it looked as if nobody could have survived the crash.

'She rang the hospital and was told they had been taken there, but would be in the operating theatre for a long time and she wouldn't be able to see them for hours. She rushed over to take care of the children. They were being looked after by social services until she got there.

'But of course it's difficult for her because of her arthritis; she can only just hobble about. She says she can't possibly look after them for long; she can't keep up with two active toddlers, and she lives in a small flat; there really isn't room for the children.'

'I'll have them,' Kit said, without needing to think about it. 'Molly is quite right—in her condition she can't possibly look after those two. They're a job for Claire to manage, let alone a woman of sixty with severe arthritis. On her bad days Molly is in such pain that she can't walk at all.'

'I think she's in a lot of pain at the moment. That's why I think you should go at once, tonight.'

She stared at him, dumfounded. 'Tonight?'

'The sooner you get there the better, surely?'

'Well, yes, but . . .'

'If we travel overnight—'

' "We"?' she repeated, taken aback.

Liam shrugged offhandedly. 'It will take a good five hours to drive to Yorkshire from here with the weather that bad up north. A trip like that is far too long for you to do alone, especially by night in rain and fog. It isn't safe for a woman on her own to drive along motorways at night, you know that, but in bad weather it's madness. We'll have to take it slowly and carefully. We can take it in turns to drive.'

She was very moved by the offer. 'It's very good of you, Liam, but it really isn't necessary; I could get the train tomorrow.'

His expression revealed his impatience. 'You aren't thinking, Kit! You are going to have a lot of stuff to bring back with you—all the luggage from Paul's car, including a travel cot for little Kate. She's too young to sleep in a bed; they were bringing a collapsible cot for her. You can't possibly go by train, and your car isn't big enough. If we go in my estate car there will be plenty of room for the cot, and the children's clothes and toys.'

Stubbornly she insisted, 'That's very kind of you, but I could just buy a cot when we get back here. All they really need is a few clothes I can pack in a suitcase.'

Liam looked at her as if he wanted to shake her, his grey eyes fierce. 'Kit, these kids have had a traumatic shock—they may not be physically hurt but they're going to be very distressed. What they need is reassurance, comfort—they'll need familiar things around them. Their toys and clothes, and even the baby's cot, are all going to be vital to help them get over this. Now come on, stop arguing; just grab what you need and we'll be on our way.'

'Why do we have to leave right now? We can't walk into Molly's flat in the middle of the night and collect the kids!'

'Of course we can't, and, before you do, I'm sure you want to see Paul and Claire.' He looked down at her drily. 'But, even if you go to bed now, are you going to be able to sleep, with all this on your mind?'

She stared back, biting her lower lip. He was right, of course; she wouldn't get a wink of sleep, worrying about Paul, about Claire, about the children.

'You'll feel better if you're on your way there, and know you'll be seeing them first thing in the morning,' he said. 'We'll stop for a break and a meal halfway at a motorway service station, which will delay us for an hour, but we're going to need that break. Night driving is more tiring than driving in the daytime.'

'You've worked it all out, haven't you?' Kit was both grateful and irritated; he was running her life, giving her orders, as if she were a child herself, leaving her no options, no chance to make a decision of her own.

'I've spent hours thinking about nothing else!' he said harshly. 'While you were on that river bank with Ingram.'

She drew a shaky breath. 'All right, I feel guilty enough about not being here when I was needed—there's no need to keep rubbing it in!'

His face was hard, unforgiving. 'I hope it was worth it!'

She quivered with resentment. 'Don't sit in judgement on me! You don't have the right! All I did was go fishing for the day— what's wrong with that? It was just bad luck that this happened.'

'Go and pack a case, Kit,' he muttered. 'We'll have to stay there a few days; we can't just grab the kids and get back here. You'll want to be sure that Paul is going to be OK before we leave. So I've booked us into a motel which has family chalets— only a couple of miles from Molly's place—and told them we'll be arriving around four o'clock. I'll start off driving because I had a nap this afternoon for a couple of hours. You can take over when I'm sleepy.'

'What about the business? We can't both take time off without warning.'

'I've already settled that with Paddy; I told her we wouldn't be at work, to let anyone who has an appointment know, and to keep an eye on things until we get back. She's a very capable girl is Paddy.'

'Yes, of course she is, but—'

'Kit, will you stop arguing? Get what you need and let's go.'

She looked helplessly at him and gave up. When Liam had made up his mind about something you had no hope of changing it or deflecting him, any more than you had of stopping a tank in full charge.

'OK,' she said with resignation. 'Has anyone told Hugh?'

'Hugh?' Liam looked blank. 'Oh, your ex-husband...of course, I should have got in touch with him. I completely forgot about him, I'm afraid.'

'I'll ring him now—I know he'll want to come over to see Paul if it is really serious.' Kit walked over to the phone and picked it up. 'I hate giving bad news over the telephone.'

CHAPTER SEVEN

THEY had been driving for nearly two hours, with Kit lying back in the passenger seat, a rug over her, her eyes shut while she tried to get some sleep, but she couldn't relax; her mind wouldn't let go of the deep anxiety possessing her. She was desperate to get to Paul. Why didn't Liam drive faster? The car seemed to move at a snail's pace.

She opened her eyes and saw the rain beating down around them, the wet greasiness of the road, the blurred dazzle of lights from streetlamps, from the cars ahead and behind, and was forced to realise that it would be dangerous to go any faster than they were.

Liam was a very good, very safe driver; his black-leather-gloved hands firmly gripped the wheel, all his attention given to what he was doing.

Her heart ached as she watched him, and he suddenly turned his head to glance at her as if becoming aware that she had her eyes open.

A flush crept up her face; self-consciously she rushed into speech. 'Where are we?'

'Not far from Nottingham. Can't you sleep?' His voice sounded husky. Had he picked up on what she was feeling?

'No; would you like me to take over the driving?'

'No, I'm fine. Try to sleep, Kit. I'm not tired but you must be.'

She closed her eyes again, but her mind was still far too busy. She kept going over what he had told her about the accident, about Paul's injuries, about Claire... Then suddenly she remembered what he had said about having booked a family chalet at a motel for them.

A family chalet. Her eyes flew wide open. 'A family chalet?' she said aloud, angrily, and Liam looked round again, frowning.

'What?'

'You said you'd booked a family chalet at a motel.'

'Yes, that's right.'

'What does that mean exactly? How many rooms in this chalet?'

'They told me that there's a sitting room, with a cooking area, a bathroom, and a bedroom with several beds in it.'

'A bedroom?' repeated Kit, red with rage. 'Just one?'

His mouth twisted with sardonic amusement. 'They don't do chalets with more than one bedroom; this isn't the Ritz!'

The smile made her even angrier. 'If you think you're sleeping in the same room as me, forget it!'

'Don't worry,' he said coolly. 'I'll sleep on the sofa in the sitting room—it turns into a bed.'

'I don't care what it turns into! You aren't sleeping on it. When we get there you can book yourself into another chalet!'

Liam glared at her, rage glittering in his grey eyes. 'Oh, go to sleep!'

She shut her eyes again, knowing that she was far too angry to be able to sleep, but the next time she opened her eyes, when the car jolted and slowed, she found that they were parking at a motorway service station. She must have slept; she had slid sideways and her head was pillowed against Liam's shoulder.

She sat up hurriedly, flushed and breathless. 'Where are we?'

'Close to Leeds—not far to York now. I need to stretch my legs; my attention was wandering. The last thing we need is another motorway crash!' He got out of the car and she threw aside her rug and scrambled out too, collecting her handbag before he locked the car.

'You should have woken me up; I could have taken over.'

'You were fast asleep; I hated to wake you.' Liam's eyes were coldly mocking. 'You looked so comfortable.'

She hurriedly turned away from that look, deeply self-conscious. Her body felt heavily lethargic from sleep. She shivered in the biting March wind. It was much colder in the north. She looked at her watch; it was after two in the morning. No wonder it was cold! She buttoned up her thick anorak and put up the hood.

They walked quickly to the restaurant complex and separated to find the toilet blocks. Before rejoining Liam Kit looked at herself in the mirror and groaned. What did she look like? Hair all over the place, face without make-up.

She splashed her face with cold water to wake herself up, patted it dry with paper towels, combed her hair back, and put on a little light make-up. She felt more human after that.

Liam scrutinised her when they met, his brows lifting in wry comment on the change in her appearance. 'Feeling better?'

'I feel more awake, anyway,' she said defiantly, and walked ahead of him into the cafeteria. She collected a tray and queued at the self-service counter for coffee and orange juice.

'The rolls just arrived; they're still hot,' said the woman at the till, pointing to a pile of crusty, golden rolls.

Kit decided not to bother but Liam leant over to pick up two of them, added several pats of butter and a tiny pot of marmalade.

There were very few people around—only half a dozen tables were occupied. Kit chose one by the window overlooking the motorway. Lorries still thundered past but there weren't many cars on the road at this hour.

Liam drank some coffee, then he spread a roll with butter and marmalade and bit into it.

'Mmm, that's really good—I love hot bread; just the smell of it makes me hungry. Have one, Kit. You need the blood sugar. That's probably why you're on such a short fuse.'

'I am not on a short fuse,' she said, picking up her glass of orange juice. She drank some and put down the glass, sighing. 'I needed that more than I needed anything else. I'll feel more human now.'

'Well, that will be a relief!' he said ironically, and she made a face at him.

Leaning back in her chair, she stared at the strange yellow glow in the sky—a reflection from the streetlamps along the motorway. It blanketed out the stars and moon; she was glad that the sky above her home town didn't have that unreal colour.

Glancing at Liam, she said, 'I just thought...how am I going to manage about my job? If I'm looking after the children I can hardly bring them to work with me, and if they're going to be with me for weeks or even months it's going to be a problem for you.'

Liam didn't look concerned; his face was calm. 'You'll have to get some help with them obviously. I've already thought it over.' She might have known he would have! 'You'll have to find a good nursery school. I've heard that the one in the church hall at the end of our street is very well run. If there's any problem you'll only be two minutes away, so if you can get them in there it would be perfect. You can drop the kids off there on your way to work and collect them at lunchtime.'

'But what about the afternoons?'

'A half-day is probably as much as they can stand—kids of their age only have so much energy and concentration—so you'll just have to work part-time while the children are with you.'

Kit gave him an uncertain look. 'That will leave the burden of the business to you, though.'

'I'll manage.' He sounded unworried. He had finished his roll and was drinking his coffee, frowning down at the speeding lights on the road below them. 'I thought I might take someone on for the afternoons while you're off.'

The casual tone alerted her. 'Anyone in mind?' she just as casually enquired, buttering a roll before biting into it.

He didn't look at her. In a slow, considering voice he murmured, 'Well, Cary could be useful. Obviously her expertise is limited to clocks, but I've discovered that she knows a considerable amount about furniture too.'

Cary. She had known it would be Cary Burnaby. Who else?

'I see,' she said, forcing herself to eat some of the warm roll although her throat was rough with jealousy and it was like swallowing powdered glass.

'Of course, she may not agree. She's very busy trying to build up custom in the shop again. A lot of old Burnaby's clients went elsewhere when he died; she has to get them back if she can. But she did tell me that money was a bit tight, so I hope she'll consider my suggestion.'

'Oh, I'm sure she will,' Kit said with bitter sarcasm. Was he kidding? Cary Burnaby would probably jump at the offer; it would give her a chance to spend a lot more time with him.

Liam's eyes narrowed on her face. 'You sound very acid. What's the matter with you? Don't you like Cary?'

'I hardly know her. It's you who'll have to work with her, not me.' She finished her coffee and looked at her watch. 'We've been here half an hour! Shall we go? I'll drive the rest of the way to give you a rest.'

'I'm fine; no need to worry about me.'

She went to the driver's side, though. 'We agreed we would share the driving.' She held out her hand. 'Keys, please.'

The rain had begun again; it ran down her face like tears as Liam glared at her.

'I'm not happy about you driving in this weather. The roads are like rivers and this car needs very careful handling. It's a big, powerful car.' He unlocked the driver's door. 'Get in the other side, Kit. You aren't driving.'

'Oh, for heaven's sake,' she burst out. 'Don't be so irritating! I'm just as capable a driver as you are!'

'But this is my car and I know how it reacts in weather like this!' He opened the door and before she could move was inside the car, behind the wheel, slamming the door behind him.

Kit couldn't just stand there getting soaked through to her skin. She felt like stamping her feet but that would be too childish. She walked round the car and got into the passenger seat, giving Liam a stare of pure dislike.

'One of these days . . .'

'Yes—what?' he mocked, laughing.

'One of these days someone will murder you,' she muttered, shivering in her wet coat.

'Meaning you?' He leaned towards her and she stiffened, green eyes wide.

'Don't you touch me!'

'If I wanted to I would!' he drawled, his hand coming out.

Her heart leapt into her mouth, but he simply grabbed her seatbelt and pulled it across her. 'I'm not driving away until you've got your seatbelt on!'

He clicked it home and straightened, looking into her furious eyes. Very softly, his lips hardly moving to let the words out, he said, 'Don't threaten me, Kit—you'd only wish you hadn't.'

She believed him. When he looked like that Liam could be very frightening.

'Where's the rug?' He leaned over the seat into the back of the car, and she watched the powerful bend of his body, her mouth going dry. The line of his back, the long legs had a disastrous effect on her pulse rate.

Ignore it! she told herself furiously, making herself listen to the rain beating down on the top of the car with a drumming sound that shut out every other noise.

She couldn't hear or see a thing outside the car; rain cascaded down over the windscreen, making the glass look like rippling skin. She was deeply conscious of being alone with him in the rain, in the darkness; it was like being in another world—one which nobody else inhabited.

He turned round, the tartan rug in his hand, and she hurriedly took it from him before he could tuck her in as if she were a child.

'Thanks,' she muttered huskily.

She felt him watching her and didn't look up to meet his eyes. If only she could hide what was happening inside her, but he knew her too well; he was as familiar with the responses of her mind and body as she was herself.

Liam knew why her hands were trembling as she pushed the rug down around her legs; he knew why she was breathing fast, her skin pale and her eyes dilated with passion. Their proximity in the confined space of the car, their isolation from the rest of the world made her vulnerable, and he knew it as well as she did.

She was waiting on tenterhooks for him to reach out again, touch her, kiss her.

If he did she knew she would cave in like hollow meringue. At this strange hour of the night, in this strangely intimate situation she no longer felt strong enough to say no. She wanted him so much it was like dying.

When Liam suddenly started the engine it was an odd shock; she felt her nerves jump as if she had touched a live wire.

He isn't interested, she thought in anguish. Not in me, not any more. I'm yesterday's news. He has other prey in view: Cary Burnaby. She's so much younger than he is, so much younger than me—that makes her a challenge to him, and he needs a challenge every so often, to persuade himself that he's still young.

Isn't that what this is all about? Isn't that why Liam doesn't want to marry again? Because if he were married he would have to settle for just one woman again, settle for a life of routine and habit, when what he is desperate for is to live like a young stud who can have any woman he wants. Liam hates the idea of growing old; he is afraid to stop running in case time catches up with him.

She glanced sideways through her lashes at him, her heart aching. But it will, Liam, she thought. Time always catches up; you can't outrun it.

Everything has its season, Liam, she wanted to say to him—being born, growing up, falling in love, having children, growing old. That's the natural round of the seasons of the human race—we begin, we end, and in between we do the best we can.

We can't make ourselves eighteen again when we are fifty. We can do a make-up job; with luck we can make ourselves look years younger; we can wear the latest fashions; but underneath them the bones and muscles of the body have lost their suppleness and elasticity. Sooner or later you have to accept that.

Oh, Liam would undoubtedly say to her, Come off it, Kit, all women want to stay looking young, and work at it! And it was true, but women were rarely driven to keep proving themselves by new conquests the way men were. That was against their very nature.

The heart is the centre of a woman's world, not the body, she thought. Women give birth to the next generation, nourish and protect it, but above all love it. A child needs love as much as it needs food and it is a woman's instinct to give it that love; that

is why women are driven not by their emotions but
by their instincts.

Women are closer to nature's heart, more down-
to-earth than men—they have always needed to love
and be loved because they understand the necessity
of love.

'What are you brooding over now?' Liam asked
her, and she shook her head, startled out of her
thoughts.

The heater was on; the car was very warm now;
her eyelids grew heavy; she drifted back to sleep.

The next time she woke up the car was stationary
and she was alone; for a second she felt a sense of
panic. Where was Liam?

Rain was still pelting down. Kit sat up and saw
him running away from the car through the rain
into a brightly lit foyer, saw a red neon sign flashing
on and off above the entrance.

They had reached the motel. She looked at the
car clock; it was half past three in the morning.

A man in a navy blue shirt leaned over a counter
to talk to Liam. He was broad-shouldered, raw-
boned, with grizzled hair—the hotel night porter,
presumably.

From what Kit glimpsed of him he was watching
Liam warily. This was an odd hour of the night to
arrive at a hotel. No doubt he was suspicious; you
couldn't blame him. She saw Liam gesturing to the
car, then saw the other man shaking his head,
shrugging.

Was Liam asking for another chalet for himself?
Kit looked around and saw simple, one-storey,

white-painted buildings on each side of the driveway. It was not a large place; she counted around a couple of dozen chalets, nicely landscaped among trees, with shuttered windows and bright, yellow-painted doors, each one with a light right outside it for security. Outside many of the chalets stood a parked car.

It looked as if they were mostly occupied. Her heart sank. What was she going to do if there wasn't a chalet free?

Liam came running back and dived into the car, rain trickling down his face.

'Did you get another chalet for yourself?'

He didn't look at her, his expression tight. 'They're all taken,' he muttered.

What was wrong with him now? 'You did ask, I suppose?'

He looked at her then, his eyes seething. 'When have I ever lied to you? Go in and ask him yourself if you don't believe me.'

She flushed at his angry tone. She couldn't blame him for resenting having his word doubted.

'Sorry.'

'So I should think!'

'It's just that ... you seemed odd.'

'Maybe that's because the night manager thought it was very funny that you wouldn't share my chalet, and started giving me advice on how to handle a woman.' He gave her a hard look. 'I don't enjoy being made to look a fool, OK?'

He started the engine again and drove along the right-hand block of chalets until he reached the one at the end—the only one that didn't have a car parked outside.

He switched off the engine and they sat there with the rain rattling down on the car roof, staring at the low building.

'Well, are we going to sit here all night?' he demanded, opening his door. He dived out into the rain and ran to the front door of the chalet, unlocked it, switched on an electric light inside, left the door open and dashed back to the car, opened the boot and began getting their two cases out. Kit, who had got out of the car and was standing waiting for him, picked up hers and hurried inside with it.

The floor plan of the single-storey chalet was simple. The front door opened into a tiny hallway from which three other doors opened out. One was open, revealing a pale green bathroom. The door on the left of that led into the bedroom; through the other she saw a long, narrow sitting room, one end of which was a little kitchen area.

Kit walked into the bedroom and put down her case to look around. There was a double bed at one end of the room, flanked by two very functional bedside tables; along a wall was a counter with a mirror above it and a telephone on it; halfway along it you walked into a chest of drawers which doubled as a room divider, and beyond that was an alcove in which were two narrow wooden bunk beds.

Everything was very clean and neat. The walls, curtains, bedspreads and lampshades were in muted colours—pale creams and greens. All the wood was a pale yellow pine.

Liam stood behind her, looking around. 'Inspirational!' he declared, grimacing. He hated modern furniture of this type—featureless, mass-produced, cheap.

She sighed. 'Well, at least it's clean.' She walked into the sitting room, which was furnished just as blandly and sparsely. There were a couple of narrow armchairs and a matching couch which must have been the sofa bed that Liam had mentioned.

He followed her; they both stared at the wooden arm rests and green striped weave of the upholstery.

'It looks about as comfortable as a bed of nails,' he said, walking over to examine it more closely. 'I suppose this is how it operates.' He jumped back suddenly with a grunt of surprise as the body of the bed shot outwards, almost knocking him over.

'It's more like a camp-bed,' he said furiously, and it was undeniably very near the ground. He looked down at it with disfavour. 'Oh, I shall have a wonderful night on this!'

'I'll take it,' said Kit.

'No, you won't,' he bit out. 'The children will be sharing your room from tomorrow. I'll have to have this bed.'

'Maybe you could book into a York hotel tomorrow? There must be lots of them; this is a major tourist centre. Hang on, I'll go and look for some blankets and a pillow.'

She went back into the bedroom. There was no spare bedlinen that she could see so she stripped one of the bunk beds and brought him an armful of sheets, a pillow and a thin duvet.

She dumped them on the sofa bed. 'Will this be warm enough? You can have another duvet. Tomorrow we'll ask the manager for some blankets. You must be exhausted. You'd better get some sleep. I'll make up the bed for you.'

He helped her grimly, not speaking, and she felt very guilty. Poor man, he had driven all this way while she'd slept comfortably in the seat beside him, and now she was making him sleep on this contraption.

Trying to placate him, she offered, 'Would you like me to make you a hot drink?'

He shrugged. 'If you can find anything! I don't imagine they stock the kitchen with groceries!'

She hurried into the kitchen area and explored the neat pine units. There was a tray inside one which held a teapot and coffee-pot, an electric kettle, cups and saucers, a selection of teabags, instant coffee, instant hot chocolate, some vacuum-packed little pots of long-life milk and several packets of biscuits.

'You were wrong about them!' she told Liam, showing him the choice they had.

'Hot chocolate,' he decided. 'While you're making it I'll use the bathroom and get ready for bed. We'll have to be up by eight to have breakfast and drive over to Molly's flat to take over the children.'

He vanished into the bathroom and a moment later she heard a shower running.

The intimacy of that made her even more edgy. She hurriedly made the hot chocolate, left Liam's on the small coffee-table in the middle of the room, and carried hers into the bedroom and locked the door.

She unpacked and put away her clothes, found her alarm clock and set it for eight o'clock, took off her clothes and put on a towelling robe, then sat on her bed sipping her chocolate, yawning. Liam didn't take long to shower; she heard him brushing his teeth and then the door of the bathroom opened.

He paused next to her door. 'It's all yours now,' he said quietly. 'I'll ring the manager and ask him for a wake-up call at eight.'

'I've got an alarm clock; I've already set it.'

'OK, then, wake me up when it goes off. Goodnight, Kit.'

'Goodnight,' she said, managing to sound calm and unflurried although she was nothing of the kind.

The sitting-room door closed and she shut her eyes, breathing raggedly.

She didn't know how she was going to bear this enforced intimacy for as much as a single night! But it would be much easier once they had the children in the chalet and weren't alone here any more.

The bathroom was steamy and warm, the mirrors cloudy. She was dying to have a shower herself; she dropped off her robe and stepped into the narrow cubicle. That was when she discovered that there wasn't enough hot water left. Liam had used it all up. The water was now lukewarm; she had to have a very quick shower, shivering.

Typical! she thought grimly, brushing her teeth before hurrying back to the bedroom. The light under Liam's door was out; he must be in bed by now. She put on her warm pink nightdress and dived under the duvet. Within minutes she was fast asleep.

Her alarm clock seemed to go off five minutes later. Blinking and disorientated, she groped for the clock and switched it off, then lay back in the blessed silence, staring around the room, which was full of grey morning light, realising where she was and what had happened the night before.

She slid out of bed, put on her dressing-gown and ran a brush over her tousled hair before she tiptoed to the bathroom. There was no sound from Liam.

She used the bathroom and then tapped on his door, but there was no response. She tapped again, louder. 'Liam!'

Still not a sound. She tried a third time, even louder. 'Wake up, Liam, it's eight o'clock.'

He didn't respond at all. She couldn't hear a sound from the room. That was when she began to get worried. She turned the handle and the door opened; she slowly pushed it wide and stared across the sitting room. On the sofa bed there was a mound; she recognised her coat and Liam's coat piled up on top of the duvet she had taken from the bunk beds.

Below all that was a long outline topped by a rumpled head of silver-streaked hair. 'Liam!' she yelled and the body didn't move.

She stood there listening. She couldn't hear him breathing. Her heart thumped with sudden fear. He wasn't breathing! He had pushed himself last night, driving all that way through the night, refusing to let her take over. He wasn't a young man any more, however much he might deny it. Why had he been so stupid, so obstinate?

That ego of his, of course! He was always trying to prove something.

She ran over to the bed, knelt down beside it, pulled back the bedclothes and there was his face— eyes shut, skin flushed, his lips parted in regular, quiet breathing.

Kit closed her eyes, weak with relief, then as her fear subsided she began to get angry. She grabbed his shoulder and shook him crossly. 'Liam, wake up! Wake up, damn you!'

His lids fluttered upwards; he gazed blankly at her. 'What? Kit? What on earth...?'

'It's eight o'clock and I've been trying to wake you up for ages. I thought you were dead or something! Just get up, will you?'

She began to get to her feet, but Liam's hand shot out and caught hold of hers, tugging her downwards again. Off balance, she fell across him with a cry of shock.

'What do you think you're doing? Don't you dare!' she burst out, the breath knocked out of her. She tried to struggle up again, only to find herself being manhandled sideways, her shoulders pinned to the bed by his powerful hands. Eyes wide and dilated with shock, she glared up at him. 'Let go of me, damn you!'

That was when she discovered that he had slept naked. The shock of seeing his long, lean body was like a violent blow; she began to shake and couldn't stop looking at him—at the wide, strong shoulders, the powerful chest, the flat stomach and slim hips, the dark, rough curls of hair springing between his thighs.

He was watching her staring. His breathing quickened; a dark flush crept up his face. His voice hoarse, he whispered, 'Don't shout at me, Kit. I don't like it.'

She dragged her gaze away from his body and looked up at his face. He was staring at her mouth. She could scarcely breathe.

'W-we...we're s-supposed to be in a hurry; w-we've got to get ready,' she stammered.

He leaned over her, his head slowly lowering, and her pulses went crazy, beating fiercely in her neck, her wrists, between her breasts.

She gave a sharp, panicky groan. 'No, Liam. It's over, you know that; I'm not letting you touch me again; I won't—'

His mouth silenced her, moving hotly.

I won't let him get to me, I won't; he isn't doing this to me, not again, she kept telling herself, repeating the words like a mantra which might protect her.

But her blood had begun to run like wildfire through her veins; she felt a deep, burning ache spreading through her body. It seemed an eternity since he had last made love to her; frustration had been eating at her for weeks and she was dying to touch him, to let her hands wander the way her eyes had just done, exploring every part of his body.

Liam's hand pushed her dressing-gown lapels apart and slid inside; she felt the warmth of it moving on her breast, his long fingers caressing and stroking. Feverishly she pushed it away and pulled her head back to mutter fiercely at him, 'No, stop it.'

His head went downwards, his mouth sliding over her throat, her shoulders, her breasts, his tongue moving sensually over her nipples, sending shivers of pleasure through her.

In panic she cried out, 'Don't . . . don't . . .'

His other hand pushed her nightdress hem upwards and silkily explored her thighs, his fingers sliding inwards into the moist, warm depths between them.

She gave a wild cry, arching mindlessly in primitive arousal, her eyes closing at last. Liam slid between her parted thighs; she heard his fierce breathing, and then he was inside her.

CHAPTER EIGHT

AFTERWARDS she began to cry, silently, tears rolling down her face. Liam turned over to look at her. 'Kit! What's the matter? Don't, Kit,' he muttered, his arms going round her and pulling her into his body.

It was warm and comforting to be in his arms, his hand stroking up and down her back, but she pushed him away, her whole body shaking with her sobs.

'No, leave me alone. How could you do that? I told you I didn't want to have sex with you again. How could you do that?' The intensity of their lovemaking was still reverberating inside her; it had been a little like dying, the wild release of weeks of frustration. She had needed it badly, but she was angry with herself for having given in to her need, for having allowed him to seduce her into bed.

She had been so determined not to let him make love to her again until she was sure that he loved her enough to offer her more than the most basic sensual pleasure, but he had only had to touch her and she had surrendered. She despised herself.

He caught her chin in his hand and tipped her face up so that he could see it, his grey eyes staring into hers.

'I love you, Kit,' he said, and she felt as if he had hit her—the shock was that agonising. 'And you love me, don't you? You can't deny it. Not after we made love like that. We were always good together, but that wasn't just good—it was out of this world. So don't say you don't love me, Kit. You do, and I love you.'

'Not enough!' she threw at him in anguish. 'Don't use those words when you don't mean them!'

'I mean them, Kit!' he insisted fiercely.

She shook her head. 'No, you only love me when it's convenient for you—when you want to have sex with me, when you want someone to go to a film with, when I am useful to you in other words. You don't love me all the time. You don't want me in your home, in your life, except on your terms.'

'You've got it all wrong, Kit,' he groaned. 'I want you. My God, don't you know I want you badly, every minute of every day? I've been so jealous of Ingram that I've hardly slept for the last few weeks. I can't eat; I can't think.'

'Jealousy isn't love either,' she flared. 'It's just possessiveness, and I hate that. You have no right to feel possessive when you don't want to stand up in front of everyone and say I belong to you and you belong to me.'

He gave a deep sigh. 'You don't understand, Kit...'

'How can I when you won't tell me what's wrong?'

She felt his tension and lay still, no longer crying but her face wet with her tears, praying that he would talk to her at last. Now that she knew about his wife she thought she understood why he was so reluctant to commit himself, but she could be wrong; there could be some other reason why he didn't want to share his life with her. While he kept so many secrets locked away what sort of future could they have?

She looked at him pleadingly. 'Liam...tell me...' But he was silent, still hesitating; she felt him arguing with himself, fighting the same battle between his feelings and his fear.

'I don't even know where to start,' he muttered, then reached over for a box of paper tissues on the bedside table, pulled one out and dried her face as if she were a child. 'I hate to see you cry, darling; whatever you may think you mean the world to me; I never wanted to hurt you, but I'm afraid of getting hurt myself.'

'I would never hurt you, Liam!' she whispered.

'I know you wouldn't want to, and the rational part of me knows there's no reason why you should, but every time I think about making our relationship permanent I get this feeling of panic; I'm terrified—' He broke off. 'Look, it will take too long to explain, and we've got to get up and get ready.' He shifted in the bed as if he was going to get out of it and she put a hand up and caught his wrist.

'Don't stop now, Liam! If you do you'll probably never talk to me, and that's the whole problem between us. You've never talked to me about anything important, any part of your life that isn't an open book to the whole world!'

'That's ridiculous! Of course I have!'

'No, Liam. I sometimes think you're a total stranger to me, that I don't know who you are. I even wonder if you know yourself. The way you act is so contradictory; I'm so confused about you—and I think you're confused too.'

'Confused as hell,' he agreed, closing his eyes. 'I've spent so many years hiding the truth away, lying, pretending. I don't know how to stop, Kit.'

'It's not as hard as you think—just start somewhere, anywhere. Tell me about Claudia.'

His lids lifted and he looked sharply at her. 'You've always known that Claudia was the core of the problem, haven't you? You were always trying to get me to talk about her, asking me questions... Was that guesswork, or have you heard rumours, gossip?'

She shook her head, her eyes compassionate. Even now he was afraid of people knowing! After all this time, when Claudia had been dead for so long!

'I've never heard a whisper about her. But you were so reluctant to talk about her that of course I was curious; I knew you were hiding something; I just didn't know what it was.'

He turned on to his back and lay staring at the ceiling. 'I couldn't bear to tell you, Kit. You're right—this is all about Claudia. She taught me not to trust my own mind or my instincts; she made my life such hell that I swore I'd never let myself get into the hands of a woman again. It's hard to explain how trapped I felt, and how desperately I wanted to be free—so desperately that I couldn't bring myself to marry again, or even live with a woman again, however much in love I was.'

Her heart leapt and she closed her eyes.

Liam was still staring at the ceiling, unaware of her. Grimly he went on, 'I was crazy about her in the beginning, when we first met. She was so beautiful when she was seventeen—fragile even then, but very sweet and very feminine. She didn't talk much; she was shy and sensitive, and I felt sorry for her because her father was a notorious local drunk.'

Kit stared at him in shock. Geraldine hadn't mentioned that; had she known about her grandfather?

Liam went on flatly, 'He had drunk himself out of a job by the time I got to know Claudia, and the family were in terrible straits; he had no money so God knows where he got his drink from, but he was always drunk when I saw him. It must have been a terrible ordeal for her and her mother; everyone in town knew, but she never talked about him to me, and I carefully avoided mentioning him to her. He died of liver failure a couple of months after we met so I never really knew him very well. Claudia and I got married about six months later.'

'Were you happy?'

'At first, yes. My parents gave us a deposit on a house for our wedding present, and we were in heaven for the first couple of years, but then Claudia got pregnant and she changed... Pregnancy made her ill and she was a different girl. Her mother moved in with us to take care of her.'

'That can't have been easy—having your mother-in-law living with you.'

Liam turned his head and gave her an ironic smile. 'In fact it made our lives much easier. Claudia wasn't very good at running a house anyway, not that that mattered to me at the time; we were both very young and we just wanted to have fun. I didn't mind the house being in a muddle at first, but once she was pregnant she didn't do anything at all—the house wasn't cleaned, food wasn't cooked; I got more and more fed up, but what could I do?

'She wasn't very strong; she kept having headaches, being ill. As I said, it was a bad pregnancy. Everything that could go wrong went wrong for her—she had terrible morning sickness, she couldn't sleep, she couldn't keep food down. I was at my wits' end, so when her mother offered to move in I was relieved; I jumped at the offer. Her mother took care of her and the house and my life improved enormously after that.'

'Did Claudia have any brothers or sisters?'

'No, she was an only child; her mother had had three or four miscarriages before Claudia was born. She was a small, pale, thin woman who never spoke much; she never told me what she was thinking, but I realised later that she had been worried about

Claudia from the minute I'd married her, although she didn't tell me why.'

Kit was puzzled. 'What was she worried about? Was she afraid that Claudia was going to have the same problems having children?'

'No, it wasn't that. She watched her like a hawk, and I just thought she was a possessive mother; I thought she smothered Claudia. It was only when Claudia was expecting Geraldine that I began to suspect something was really wrong with her, but even then I didn't guess the truth. I was a blind fool.'

'It's always hard to work out other people, especially if they're hiding things and you don't know what's going on,' Kit said drily, and he gave her a wry glance.

'OK, I take the point—I should have tried to talk to you before, and I meant to but but I kept putting it off.'

'Never put off till tomorrow what you can do today, my father always used to say!' she said, half-smiling, and Liam grimaced.

'He was right, absolutely right; I should have forced myself to talk to you. But I was still recovering from years of living a lie, Kit. I wasn't ready to tell the truth to anyone. That was the worst thing Claudia did to me—taught me to lie to everyone.

'She lied to me. From very early on in our marriage. That was something else I worked out later. She started drinking in secret—after Felix was born, I think. I never knew quite when it started.

'Her mother knew, of course; she protected her, helped her hide the truth—at first I blamed her bitterly for that, but she loved Claudia more than life itself; all the poor woman was trying to do was stop what was going on, but she couldn't, and she was terrified that once I knew I'd throw Claudia out, that I'd end the marriage and that would be a disaster Claudia might never recover from. Her husband had lost his job, ruined his life and theirs; she was afraid Claudia was going down the same road.'

'Poor woman,' murmured Kit, thinking of her own child. 'I wonder what I'd have done in her place? If this had happened to Paul...I don't know; it's so easy to say you'd do this or that, but if you haven't been in that position how can you know what you'd do?'

'Yes, that's true. But she should have told me— if I'd known sooner I might have got help for Claudia, but by the time I did the drink had a hold on her.'

Kit watched him sympathetically and he gave her a grim, brooding look.

'It is a sickness, you know, alcoholism—if you get it in your blood it's very hard to fight. If I'd known that before I married Claudia I might have been able to help her, but I knew nothing about alcoholism then.

'When I first found out that Claudia was drinking secretly I flew into a terrible temper with her. I was so dumb that I actually thought I only had to tell her, Stop it! and she would. Of course she was just more careful not to let me find out; she went on drinking when I was at work. But she couldn't keep it secret when I was in the house; within a few months I knew she was still drinking, and that was when I took her to see the doctor, and it began to dawn on me just how serious it was.'

'Had she had Geraldine by then?'

He nodded. 'The children were very small, though. Felix was just about to start school and Geraldine was a toddler. Her mother took care of them; at least I didn't need to worry about them while she was around.'

'If only she'd told you, though!'

He sighed. 'Yes. She was a very stupid woman, but Claudia was her whole world. She went on protecting her even when it was actually harming Claudia. I couldn't convince her she was wrong. Our family doctor sent Claudia to a clinic, and she came home a few months later apparently cured. I thought she was; maybe she thought she was—but within a year she was secretly drinking again.'

'But why, Liam? Why did she drink?' She met his darkened eyes and bit at the inside of her lip, but had to go on. There had been enough secrets, enough evasion; she wasn't going to hide what she was thinking. 'There must have been a trigger, there had to have been something wrong, surely?'

'I didn't beat her up,' he said harshly, 'if that's what you suspect.'

Kit was shocked, her eyes opening to their widest extent. 'Liam! Of course I don't! You're not the type.'

Ah, but what type was he, this man who had hidden so much from her although they had known each other for much of their lives? And not only from her—he had hidden the truth about his wife from the whole town. His life had been a carefully constructed façade behind which a bitter, troubled man had hidden.

'Although I wanted to later,' he grimly admitted. 'However, I didn't, Kit. I never laid a finger on her.'

She watched his dark face. There were other ways of hurting someone; you didn't need to lay a finger on them. Liam had hurt *her*, hadn't he? You could break someone's heart with a word, a look.

Gravely she said, 'Liam, there had to be a reason why she drank; something must have made her start.'

'She was unhappy,' he muttered. 'Of course she was unhappy—but why she was God only knows! Maybe she never loved me. She never told me why she was unhappy, and by the time it dawned on me that she must be I was unhappy myself.'

'You never asked her?' Kit asked incredulously.

'Of course I did! I asked until I was blue in the face, but I got no rational answers. I gave up asking in the end. By then I no longer loved her. In fact, she made me sick. I was disgusted by her. If you had ever seen her when she was drunk you'd understand.'

He shuddered, his face pale. 'I kept hoping she would be cured, but in the end I realised that she didn't want to be. Drinking was her escape from a life she found intolerable.'

Soberly Kit said, 'Maybe you should have divorced her.' She hesitated, not wanting to hurt his feelings, but she had to say it. 'Liam, maybe you were the problem. Maybe she wasn't happy with you.'

His face was grim. 'Do you think that that didn't occur to me? I even suggested a separation, with divorce in mind, but she almost went crazy when I tried to talk to her about it. She didn't want to lose the children, she said, and she knew I would never let them go—I couldn't risk it. How could I trust them with a woman who might drink herself unconscious every day?'

'But her mother would have taken care of them.'

'Her mother wouldn't have been there for ever. In fact, she died when Geraldine was about seven, and after that I got a nanny who was a trained nurse and could cope with Claudia too. She did her best to find out why Claudia was so unhappy, but she told me she didn't think even Claudia knew why she drank.'

'Maybe she was so unhappy as a child because of her father that nothing and nobody could have made her happy.'

'Who knows? She saw a lot of shrinks over the years but none of them seemed able to come up with any answers. My marriage was over many years before she died. My only concern was for the children. I spent most of my married life trying to stop people finding out about Claudia for their sake.' He paused, then added flatly, 'And my own, if I'm honest, because I just couldn't bear the idea of people knowing the truth.'

'But why couldn't you tell me? That hurts, Liam. How did you think I'd react, for heaven's sake?'

He looked at her quickly, his eyes dark. 'I couldn't bear you to know. I was ashamed; you've no idea how bad it got at times; I was afraid you would start seeing me differently.'

'But it wasn't you who drank! It was your wife.'

'I felt just as guilty. I should have found a way of curing her. I failed her.' He paused and sighed. 'And then, if you knew, I realised I'd have to make a decision about the future, and that was something else I couldn't make myself do.'

Fiercely she said, 'You were ready to lose me rather than tell me! How can you say you loved me?'

'I do, Kit!' he insisted, his eyes intense. 'It was never because I didn't love you. Really, it had nothing to do with you... I told you, I was paralysed, stricken with a terrible inability to do anything, make any decision, make up my mind about my life, my future. After Claudia finally died I just felt numb for a couple of years. My life with her had been such a nightmare that being free at last left me in a state of shock.'

She could understand that. The more she heard about his life with Claudia, the more she marvelled at the way he had hidden the truth so well for so long.

'The truth is,' Liam said thickly, 'that I was in love with you even before Claudia died, but I pushed it away; I wouldn't let myself love you.'

She was stunned; he had never told her that before.

He picked her hand up, held her palm against his cheek, his eyes half-closed. 'I felt guilty about that too. My marriage was a disaster area, but I'd always been faithful to Claudia. Then suddenly I started to think about you all the time; I counted the days until I saw you, and when I did I felt stupidly happy, like a schoolboy with a crush. I kept fighting the way I felt; I didn't want to get involved with any woman ever again.

'Then Claudia died, and your husband left you, and I didn't know how badly it had hit you. I wanted to help you get over it, so I offered you that job; then you became my partner and I saw you every day, and the more I saw of you, the more I wanted you.'

He turned his mouth into her palm, his lips moving softly, warmly on her skin. 'I love you so much, Kit. I'm sorry it has taken me so long to get around to telling you. I didn't think I could bear to get married again. I knew that was what you wanted, I knew I was hurting you, but I was scared stiff. My marriage to Claudia had been hell—I knew I'd never survive if I remarried and it all went wrong again.'

'I'm not Claudia!'

'I know, darling, but I kept wondering ... was it my fault she drank? What if I made you unhappy too?'

She put her arms around him and held him, her cheek against his bare chest, his heart beating rhythmically into her.

'Liam, that's crazy. Of course you won't.'

They lay still for a moment, then he bent his head and kissed the top of her hair.

'Forgive me, Kit.'

'I'll think about it,' she said ruefully, but she turned her face up to smile at him, her heart in her eyes. She knew she would forgive him; she loved him far too much to stay angry with him now that she knew what lay behind his doubts and uncertainties, how he felt about her, why he had delayed so long, shut her out for so long.

Huskily he asked, 'And you won't see Ingram again, will you? I can't bear it, Kit, knowing you're with him. It was torture imagining you were sleeping with him—you belong to me!'

'I never slept with him! We're friends, not lovers, Liam. I like Joe a lot, but there wasn't the remotest chance of us getting any closer than that.'

'He fancies you; I can see it in his face!'

She lowered her lashes, a faint smile on her face. 'Maybe he does, a little.'

'A lot,' Liam said. 'And stop smiling like that. You know he fancies you, and you're flattered— don't bother to deny it; it's obvious.'

She laughed openly. 'Well, I must admit... After all, I am ten years older than him; it is flattering being chased by someone so much younger and that attractive.'

'So you do think he's attractive?' he said with jealousy roughening his voice.

Kit gave him a teasing glance. 'Oh, come on, Liam, he is; you know he is!'

He lay still, frowning. 'I don't want you seeing him again.'

'I'll have to see him to explain why I can't date him any more,' she pointed out.

'Write him a letter.'

'Liam! I can't do that. It's too impersonal.'

'Ring him up, then.'

'No, I must talk to him, face to face. Poor Joe, he deserves that at least.'

'I'll come too, then.'

'Don't be ridiculous. I must see him alone.'

Liam growled, scowling. 'Well, in a public place, then—over dinner somewhere, so that there are lots of other people around. And don't let him take you home afterwards.'

'What on earth do you think he's going to do? Joe's a lovely man; he'll accept the situation when I explain.'

'I should damned well hope so,' he said, looking as if he didn't believe it.

Kit shifted to make herself more comfortable against him and caught sight of his watch with a shock of dismay.

She snatched it up and gave a wail of horror. 'It's nearly nine!'

Liam groaned. 'We'll have to get up, then.'

'We should have been on our way to Molly's by now!'

'You distracted me,' he accused, looking down at her with half-lowered lids, his eyes smouldering with passion. He bent to kiss her again; their lips met and Kit quivered, then pushed him away.

'No, Liam! We must get up.'

She slid off the bed, snatched up her clothes and fled. Over her shoulder she told him, 'I'll have the bathroom first this morning!'

'Well, don't stay in there all day!' he threw after her.

'Five minutes,' she promised, and kept her word.

Half an hour later she and Liam had breakfast in the motel coffee-shop—a light meal of orange juice, coffee and toast—after which they drove to Molly's flat.

She opened the door—a short, plump woman with a lot of greying dark hair curled like chrysanthemum petals around her warm, friendly face. Her eyes lit up as she saw them. 'Oh, Kit, thank heavens you've got here,' she said, hugging her. 'I've been at my wits' end.'

She seemed to have aged ten years since the last time Kit had seen her; her eyes were red-rimmed as if she had been crying, and she was very pale under her make-up.

'They aren't worse?' Kit broke out, her heart in her mouth.

'No, no,' Molly quickly reassured her. 'I rang up five minutes ago and the hospital said they're both improving; they can have visitors at five o'clock this afternoon.'

'Not until then?' Kit was disappointed. Molly gave her an understanding look.

'No, I'm afraid not—and we won't be able to stay long—just a few minutes. They're both still weak; they need lots of rest; I expect they're both heavily sedated.'

Kit nodded, sighing. 'It's such a worry, isn't it?'

Molly groaned. 'I had a hard job getting to sleep last night, and when I did I got woken up after just a couple of hours. Believe me, I've had a terrible night. Kate kept waking up, crying for her mother. Poor little mite, she doesn't really understand what's happening, and she misses Claire. I lost a lot of sleep and I'm feeling like grim death. I love them, you know that, but I'm not a young woman any more; I can't keep up with them. My arthritis is much worse than usual if I don't get enough sleep.'

'You look very pale, Molly,' Kate said sympathetically. 'You need a long rest; it must have been a nightmare for you, worrying about Claire and having to cope with the children too.'

'It hasn't been easy,' the other woman agreed. She turned to smile at Liam. 'Hello, nice to see you again. It's very good of you to come with Kit— whatever time did you leave Silverburn to get here at this hour of the morning?'

'We drove up overnight—we're staying at a motel just outside the city. Kit felt you would be under a strain, what with your arthritis and trying to take care of two very lively kids.'

Molly grimaced. 'A strain? That's an understatement. Last night was a real ordeal. Of course Kate is full of beans this morning. She and Ian woke up at seven, demanding their breakfast, and now they're playing a very noisy game under the sitting-room table.'

Kit could hear them. She smiled. 'I'll go and see them, shall I? Look, why don't you go back to bed and try to catch up with your sleep? I'll see to the children.'

'Are you sure? They are a handful, Kit. They have so much energy it's frightening.'

Kit laughed. 'I'll cope, don't worry. Thank heavens I don't. have arthritis like you, although I'm starting to get twinges in my knees on wet days.'

'Well, take care not to overtire yourself, and wake me up if there's a problem,' Molly said, and, leaning on her stick, hobbled away to her bedroom.

'I'll put the kettle on for coffee,' Liam said, looking around the tiny flat. 'My God, there isn't room to swing a cat, is there?'

'It's OK for one,' said Kit. 'But it must be very difficult to have two kids here. No wonder she didn't get any sleep.'

Liam opened the door into the small galley-type kitchen and Kit went into the sitting room, which was probably the largest room in the entire flat. Bloodcurdling growls and squeaks were coming from under the table, which took up a quarter of the little room.

Kit walked towards it and the growls and squeaks stopped abruptly. Two small heads poked out from under the long, fringed tablecloth; two pairs of eyes lifted to stare.

'What are you two playing? Is that a zoo under there?' she asked them, her heart clenching at the sight of the grazes and bruises on their small faces. Thank God they hadn't been more badly hurt in the crash.

'Granma!' Kate said, scrambling out.

Kit bent to hug her, and then hugged four-year-old Ian as he emerged from their hiding place too. They hugged back, their arms half strangling her.

'Mummy was hurted,' Kate said, her blue eyes enormous and anxious in her small face, watching her grandmother for any reaction. 'She's in hospital.'

'She'll get better soon and come home,' Kit promised, smiling a quick reassurance.

'When?' The two faces gazed up hopefully.

'Well, she'll have to stay in hospital for a few days, so I thought you might like to stay with me until Mummy and Daddy are all better,' she told them carefully.

'In your house?' Ian asked, clinging to one of her hands while Kate held the other, and she nodded to him.

'Yes, you'll have a little holiday with me until Mummy and Daddy come out of hospital.'

Liam came into the room and they stared at him, eyes uncertain.

'Hello, remember me?' he asked, and they shook their heads. 'I work with your grandma; you visited us, don't you remember?'

'At Granma's office?' Ian thought aloud, nodding. 'You gave us toffee apples.'

Kate beamed. 'Toffee apples,' she repeated. 'I love toffee apples.'

Liam's grey eyes met Kit's. 'Well, maybe we could go shopping and buy you some,' he suggested.

'Yes, please,' Kate said. 'Now?'

'Why not?' Liam said to Kit, 'It would probably be a good idea to get them out into the fresh air. We could find a park, have a walk, use up some of that energy.'

They left a note for Molly on her kitchen table, explaining that they were taking the children out, and then they drove to some nearby shops and picked up some essential items for the motel chalet—food for them all for a couple of days. They managed to find some toffee apples, and once they had located a small neighbourhood park they parked and took the two children to the children's play area.

After they had been on the swings and slides Ian and Kate settled down on a bench with their toffee apples and ate them in a slow, pleasurable way, comparing them at intervals to see who had eaten the most.

'What a sticky mess!' Liam commented wryly as they threw the apple cores into a nearby waste bin.

Kit cleaned their toffee-covered hands and faces and then the children had a final swing before they all drove back to Molly's flat.

While Ian and Kate sat up at the sitting-room table, crayoning and under instruction to make very little noise, Kit and Liam worked in the kitchen preparing a lunch of grilled plaice and steamed rice with sweetcorn, which the children adored, green beans, of which they were not fond at all, and grilled tomatoes, which Liam requested.

Molly must have heard them although they tried to move quietly; she came limping into the kitchen, looking much better with more colour in her face, and clearly rested.

'Had a good sleep?' asked Kit, and she nodded.

'I got nearly three hours. Thank you; I feel more human now. There hasn't been any news?'

'I rang the hospital half an hour ago and they said both Paul and Claire were doing very well. We can definitely visit them this evening, but we can't take the children, I'm afraid, and the rule is that only one of us can see them at a time. But they're in different wards, so we can swap over halfway.'

'And I'll take care of the kids while you're in the hospital,' Liam added.

Molly gave him a grateful look. 'Isn't he wonderful?'

'Isn't he, though?' agreed Kit with faint amusement as she met Liam's wry gaze.

They spent the rest of the afternoon with Molly and all drove to the hospital together at five o'clock. Liam took the children for a drive through the countryside while Kit and Molly went into the hospital. They had agreed that they would each begin with a visit to their own children and then swap over after ten minutes.

Although Kit now knew the details of Paul's injuries it was still a terrible shock to her to see him, a white collar around his neck, his shoulders and chest strapped with stiff bandages and one arm bandaged to his chest.

He looked at her ruefully as she came towards him. 'Hello, Mum. Brought me any grapes?'

She managed to laugh although she had never felt less like it in her life.

'I have, actually.' She put the bag of grapes on his bedside table and kissed him. 'How do you feel?'

'Better than I look, I expect,' he said wryly. 'Have you seen Claire?'

'Not yet. Molly is with her; we're going to change places later.'

He almost nodded then winced at the pain of moving his neck. 'Ouch, I keep forgetting the whiplash. I'm afraid it will be months before I can go back to work.'

'Never mind that. Just get better; the children miss you.' She talked about Ian and Kate, and their father listened, smiling.

'I was worried about them with Molly; she can hardly walk at all some days, you know. Thanks for agreeing to have them.'

'I'm happy to have them,' she assured him. 'But I'll have to take them back to Silverburn with me,

Paul. Molly's flat is too small for all of us to move in with her, and, anyway, I have my job; I can't take weeks off work, I'm afraid, but Liam says I can work part-time, so I'll find a good nursery school for the mornings and spend the rest of the day with the kids.

'At the weekends we could drive up here again to see you and Claire. The sister on her ward told Molly that the kids could see Claire in a few days' time when she's stronger. They can come to see you tomorrow, though, so that will reassure them.'

'Where are they now?'

'With Liam; he has taken them for a drive.'

'So Liam came with you?'

Kit blushed like a schoolgirl as her son's curious, questioning eyes rested on her, but at that moment Molly joined them.

'Time to swap over,' she said rather too brightly, as if tears weren't far away.

Kit bent to kiss her son. 'See you tomorrow, and don't worry about the children; they're going to be OK.'

When she saw Claire her shock was far worse. Her daughter-in-law was almost unrecognisable, her face swollen and puffy and bruised, pocked with red where glass had hit it, her features so distorted that it was only her eyes that Kit recognised. Her chest, like Paul's, was strapped with bandages and the bedclothes were lifted from her injured legs on a dome-shaped structure.

Weak tears trickled down her broken face as she looked at Kit. Her swollen mouth moved and a whisper came out. ''Lo...'

Kit sat down beside her and picked up her hand, managing a smile. 'Hello, Claire. Paul sends his love. The ward sister says he can ring you and have a chat tomorrow, just for a minute. He's very worried about you and wants to make sure you're OK. Ian and Kate send their love too; you can see them soon.'

Claire couldn't talk; she went on crying silently, and Kit felt like crying too. It was only now that she saw her daughter-in-law that she realised how long it would be before Claire was well enough to come back to ordinary life.

'I'll look after them; they'll be fine with me,' she promised, and Claire gave her a grateful look. 'I don't want you worrying about them,' Kit added, feeling desperately sorry for her. She knew how she would feel in Claire's place, not only feeling so ill and being in terrible pain but having to worry about her children too.

No mother liked to be parted from her small children for long. Claire must have realised that it would be a very long time before she could come home and have her children with her again.

Kit and Liam stayed up north for another couple of days, until the ward sister agreed that Claire was strong enough to stand the emotional ordeal of seeing her children. Kit talked to them in advance, explaining how ill their mother was, pleading with them to be very good, and not to cry when they saw her or they would upset her very much.

'Can she come home now?' asked little Kate, and over her head Molly and Kate exchanged sad, rueful looks.

She was too small to understand the real situation. But Claire badly wanted to see her, so they took the risk and Kit stayed with her and Ian during the brief visit, to be on hand as soon as Claire showed signs of distress or exhaustion.

The following day they drove back to Silverburn, taking the children with them. They broke the long trip up for Ian and Kate by making several stops for them to stretch their legs, wander around the motorway service station shops, go to the lavatory, drink orange juice and eat their favourite cherry muffins, but the children still found the journey tedious and exhausting. Long before they reached their destination both Ian and Kate had fallen asleep in the back of the estate car.

'Poor little mites,' murmured Kit, turning her head to watch them as they were about to reach Silverburn. 'I'm worried about this long separation from their mother, especially for little Kate; she's still a baby and she's very tearful about Claire.'

'I know, it is worrying, but there's nothing whatsoever we can do about it except try to keep her happy and busy. Once they start at nursery school they'll have more to occupy them—that should help; and at least they have you; they aren't with strangers.'

'That's true,' she agreed, then looked out of the window with a start. 'You've taken the wrong turning—this doesn't lead into town, it leads to...'

'My house.' He nodded coolly. 'And that's where we're going.'

She sat up in alarm, her body tense. 'Liam, I want to get the children fed and into bed as soon as possible; there isn't time to visit your house first.'

'It isn't a visit. You and the children are moving in with me.'

'Moving in with you?' Her heart had quickened and she was afraid to believe what she thought he was saying.

He turned his head to smile at her in a way that made it clear that he knew what was going through her mind. 'There's no more room in your little flat for two children than there is in Molly's place—but my house has plenty of space, and, even more importantly, it has a big garden, so they can spend hours out of doors, running around and using up some of that spare energy.'

Kit was stunned. Huskily she said, 'It's very kind of you, Liam, and of course it's true that I don't have much space in my flat, and it would be wonderful for them to have a garden to play in, but having two small children in your house will be very disruptive, you know; have you thought this through?'

'I like small children, always have,' he returned, smiling at her.

'But, Liam...'

'Stop arguing,' he said, pulling up outside his closed, elaborately patterned wrought-iron gates. He leaned out to press an electronic zapper in their direction, and the gates smoothly swung open. Liam drove through them. Ahead a garage door was already opening; he drove in and stopped the engine.

They carried the two children into the house; flushed and sleepy, Ian and Kate stared around, bewildered.

'This isn't Granma's,' Kate said, looking worried.

'Where are we?' asked Ian.

'This is my house; you're going to stay with me for a while,' Liam told them.

Kate gave him a wild, terrified look and clung to her grandmother's neck. 'Want to stay with Granma,' she insisted, almost strangling Kit with her tiny, clutching arms.

'Your grandma is staying too,' Liam assured her, and at that moment the sound of barking began outside, and the children's eyes widened in surprise.

'Dogs!' said Kate, staring about her in excitement. 'Dogs. Granma, there's dogs barking.'

Kit detached her clutching hands and put her down on a chair in the large, elegantly furnished drawing-room.

'Have you got dogs?' Ian eagerly asked Liam, who nodded.

'Yes, I've got two big dogs and two little ones—'

'Baby dogs?' Kate asked, eyes shining.

'Puppies?' Ian said scornfully.

'Yes, Labradors,' Liam told him. 'They live outside in kennels, but they can come in and play with you after tea until you go to bed.' He glanced at Kit. 'Why don't you take the children upstairs and show them where they're going to be sleeping? I'll bring Kate's cot upstairs and set it up, and while you're making her bed I'll bring their cases up too. Then they can have a bath and get into pyjamas while I'm making their supper.'

Two hours later the children were finally in bed and asleep, and Kit and Liam collapsed in the drawing room in front of a log fire. The dogs were back in their kennels but evidence of their presence remained—some torn scraps of paper, a dog biscuit on a chair, a ball on the smooth, pale carpet where Kate and Ian had played with the two puppies, hugging and squeezing them, laughing ecstatically as the roly-poly little creatures bounced and barked.

Here and there Kit could see golden dog hairs left by the parent dogs who had watched uneasily as the children had staggered about clutching their offspring, who had wriggled and squirmed, trying to lick them.

The puppies had been a huge success. The children had been so enraptured by them that they had gone to bed quite happily once Liam had promised that they could play with them again tomorrow.

Kit looked drily at Liam. 'Are you sure you're going to be able to put up with us here for weeks? It is quite a responsibility you're taking on.'

They had not yet put on the lights; dusk had
fallen outside and the firelight made shadows on
the ceilings, carving Liam's features into a strange
mask as he stared back at her.

He got out of his chair and came across the
hearth to where she leaned back in a corner of a
brocade-covered sofa. Kit watched him, her mouth
going dry, her heart beginning to beat far too fast,
making her breathless.

Liam sat down on the sofa, very close to her.
'I've stopped running away from responsibility,
Kit.'

'Have you, Liam?' she asked huskily, and he
smiled at her, reaching out a hand to stroke her
cheek.

'Yes. Ever since Claudia died I've been ducking
out of anything that might land me with the responsibility of another human being. I needed to
be free for a while; I thought I needed to be free
for ever, but I've realised what a lonely, empty
world I'd find myself living in! I let things drift for
far too long; I wouldn't face up to the fact that I
loved you and so I almost lost you.' He looked into
her green eyes, his face grave. 'Didn't I?'

'Maybe,' she said, not sure what might have
happened if he hadn't come back to her.

'It was when you started seeing Ingram that I
really understood how much you meant to me.' He
looked at her with a twisting, crooked smile. 'And
you meant me to understand, didn't you? You were
using Ingram to teach me a lesson. He never meant
anything to you.'

She frowned. 'I didn't use Joe! He asked me out and I accepted, but we were never more than friends, on either side. It wasn't a question of me using him.'

'I think he really fell for you,' Liam said roughly.

Kit shook her head. 'He likes me, maybe, but we never got beyond the friendship stage. Maybe we might have done if things had been different. I like him a lot, but there's a huge gap between liking and loving, Liam.'

'I hope he's going to accept that a friend is all he's ever going to be,' he said, his lips barely parting to bite the words out. 'I don't want you seeing him alone again, Kit. Whatever it was it's over. Ingram will just have to face that fact.'

'Joe is a nice man; of course he'll understand,' she said, hoping she was right. She had made Joe no promises—far from it. She had been frank with him from the first time they'd met; he couldn't say that she had ever hidden anything or lied to him.

'He'd better,' Liam said, then his long arm curled round her, pulling her closer. 'I love you; will you marry me, Kit?'

She let her body yield softly, warmly to his possessive grip. 'You don't have to marry me,' she murmured, half-teasing, half-touched. 'We can just live together—these days it doesn't have to be marriage, and at our age there aren't going to be any children so we can feel free to live any way we choose. Nobody much will care if we are married or not.'

He looked down at her, frowning. 'I thought you wanted to get married!'

'I was tired of living alone, coming back to an empty flat every night, never having anyone to share things with; it's a lonely life, Liam. I thought you loved me—you said you did—and we were sleeping together, yet you didn't want to live with me. I needed more than good sex or a few evenings out together. I needed to share my life with someone.'

'So do I,' he said softly. 'I didn't want to admit it; I kept trying to kid myself that I was fine the way I was living, but I knew all the time that I needed you, that my house was empty without you, that it would never be a home until you were in it.

'And I want to marry you, darling. You said you wanted me to stand in front of the whole world and tell them that I love you and we belong together. Well, that's what I want too. When I was scared you might go off with Ingram I realised at last just how much I wanted you.'

Kit had waited a long time to hear him say that, and it had come at last in a mood of warm contentment, a shared happiness, not in the hot blood of their lovemaking, when such a promise might have been wrung out of him and regretted later when his blood cooled down.

He looked at her urgently, pale and intense. 'So...will you marry me, Kit?'

His voice wasn't quite steady. Liam wasn't sure of her; perhaps he never would be sure again, having so nearly lost her once. Kit put her arms around his neck and lifted her mouth towards him hungrily.

'If that's really what you want.'

'You. I want you,' he said thickly, and then neither of them said anything for a very long time. They were much too busy.

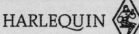